KILL ME TOMORROW: A PSYCHOLOGICAL THRILLER

BRITNEY KING

Speak of the Devil | Book Three

The New Hope Series Box Set

The New Hope Series offers gripping, twisted, furiously clever reads that demand your attention, and keep you guessing until the very end. For fans of the anti-heroine and stories told in unorthodox ways, *The New Hope Series* delivers us the perfect dark and provocative villain. The only question—who is it?

Water Under The Bridge | Book One

Dead In The Water | Book Two

Come Hell or High Water | Book Three

The Water Series Box Set

The Water Trilogy follows the shady love story of unconventional married couple—he's an assassin—she kills for fun. It has been compared to a crazier book version of Mr. and Mrs. Smith. Also, Dexter.

Bedrock | Book One

Breaking Bedrock | Book Two

Beyond Bedrock | Book Three

The Bedrock Series Box Set

The Bedrock Series features an unlikely heroine who should have known better. Turns out, she didn't. Thus she finds herself tangled in a messy, dangerous, forbidden love story and face-to-face with a madman hellbent on revenge. The series has been compared to Fatal Attraction, Single White Female, and Basic Instinct.

Around The Bend

Around The Bend, is a heart-pounding standalone which traces the journey of a well-to-do suburban housewife, and her life as it unravels, thanks to the secrets she keeps. If she were the only one with things she

wanted to keep hidden, then maybe it wouldn't have turned out so bad.
But she wasn't.

Somewhere With You / Book One

Anywhere With You / Book Two

The With You Series Box Set

The With You Series at its core is a deep love story about unlikely friends
who travel the world; trying to find themselves, together and apart.
Packed with drama and adventure along with a heavy dose of suspense, it
has been compared to The Secret Life of Walter Mitty and Love, Rosie.

COPYRIGHT

Hot Banana Press
Cover Design by Britney King LLC
Cover Image by Max Libertine
Copy Editing by Melissa Kreikemeier, 808 Editorial
Proofread by Proofreading by the Page

First Edition: 2021
ISBN 13: 9798729008605
ISBN 10: 9798729008

britneyking.com

For Jay Gatsby, whose love and outstanding lap warming skills, I could not repay even with a lifetime of puppucinnos. But I'll try, anyway.

KILL ME TOMORROW

BRITNEY KING

" Nothing spoils a good story like the arrival of an eyewitness. "
— Mark Twain

PROLOGUE

Now

I t starts out slow. The slightest twinge, coupled with an inkling that something isn't right. It quickly becomes more than that. Embarrassed, I excuse myself from the table and retreat to the bedroom, which I soon realize is a smart move.

I haven't even fully closed the door before the twinges stop and the pain takes over, engulfing me. Internal heat rages throughout my rib cage, descending downward, spiraling into my abdominal cavity. It effortlessly pulls me under until I fold in two. Thirty seconds ago, I was completely fine. Better than fine. It was the happiest moment of my life.

Now I'm dying.

Clutching my midsection in complete agony, I lean forward, pressing my body against the door, slamming it shut. I flip the lock as a cold sweat sweeps over me. Within seconds, my lungs seize. No matter how much air I attempt to suck in, it isn't enough. My vision blurs as my breath comes out in spurts. I pant like a dog on a hot day.

The room takes on a very distinct smell, reminding me of burnt flesh. It steeps the air in the combination of a liver-like scent and sulfur. While the fire may be internal, the smell isn't. My stomach knots, clenches, twists, and turns. The pain is relentless as it radiates outward, its tendrils wrapping around every inch of me. It feels like I'm being skinned alive, only from the inside out. With every inhale, the sensation tightens its grip, until I can no longer think straight.

Until I can no longer see a way out of this.

Until misery is all there is.

Whispering jumbled prayers, I pray to God, to Moses, to Buddha—I pray to anyone who will listen. I just need them to make this stop.

They don't. And it doesn't.

The searing heat engulfing my insides only intensifies. I grit my teeth so hard I fear they may chip off in my mouth. Shock forces me deep inside myself, making it hard to know what is real and what isn't. It feels like someone is prying my mouth open, holding my jaw in place, pouring battery acid down my throat. It feels like a Molotov cocktail has been buried deep within my belly. A ticking time bomb planted and detonated.

But no. It's just me in this room, alone with my poor decisions.

My mind tries to rationalize. This cannot be happening.

But it is very much happening.

As I writhe from side to side, I force myself to focus.

My eyes scan the bedroom. What can possibly save me now? My phone? *I left it in the kitchen.* Paramedics? *There isn't enough time.*

Water. What I need is water. Something, *anything*, to soothe the burning. I drag myself up, bracing my palms against my thighs. If only I hadn't been so stupid. If only I could get a handle on this.

Two steps are all it takes for me to realize what a pipe dream that is. Time slows to nothing. Internally, layers of flesh are being serrated and filleted. Slices of organs are being peeled away; shallow layers of my innards are slowly separating. Then, with a fiery explosion, what remains disintegrates into nothing. It's all happening in slow motion and I can feel everything.

A pulsating sound pings between my ears. It starts out high-pitched and shrill, and then it dims, but it plays on repeat, so I know what's coming. A cacophony of nails on a chalkboard.

If death has a sound, this is it.

I give up trying to focus on anything else. It's pointless.

My legs buckle, and my body falls to the floor with a heavy thud. The rest of me is somewhere else, halfway to hell.

This is not how this night was supposed to go.

Slinking forward, serpent-like, I inch toward the bathroom. I get nowhere fast, so I shift direction, making it to the bed, where I force myself upward. The room spins like a Tilt-A-Whirl as I sway precariously from side to side. It reminds me of my firstborn learning to walk. It reminds me of carnival trips with my children, memories that will be forgotten instead of made.

Knowing sentimentality can only get me so far, I hobble onward, still holding onto the hope that I survive to see my children's faces once again. Hoping I'll get another chance to hear them laugh. Although I know I probably won't. Right now, there is only one goal: to find water.

It won't save me. But it might buy me some time.

The bathroom is the wrong call, I realize, as I grip the inside of the doorframe. I dig my fingernails into the wood, thinking I should have gone through with the remodel. What an unforgiving place to die.

I hadn't thought the misery could get worse.

I was wrong.

The contractions deep in my gut continue to sweep over me, crashing like tall waves, each one worse than the one before.

Eventually, I lose my handle on the doorframe and with it, my footing. I fall forward, endlessly forward, until my skull hits the edge of the sink and a hard crack ensues.

I'd hoped it would end there, but it doesn't. Instead, I am witness to my suffering, as everything slows. This could just as easily be happening to someone else, and if it weren't for the relentless tearing in my stomach, maybe I could pretend that it was.

The blood though, I can't ignore. It trickles out of the corner of my mouth, vibrant against the white marble floor. Brick red and sweet, it coats my lips. I inhale the metallic scent; the warmth brings me comfort. Everything is so cold.

My mouth fills, and as I spit blood onto the floor, I see that in the fall, I've bitten off a sliver of my tongue. It looks out of place lying there all pink and moist, covered in tiny bumps. My fingers reach out to touch it. It feels muscular and rough, like something I might have once fished out of the ocean. I cup it in the palm of my hand. For what reason, I don't know. To save it? Just in case? What a silly thought. A last vestige of hope.

My cheek pressed against the cold tile, I think, *so this is where it ends*. There's a rattling in my chest, the kind you hear stories about.

It tells me I don't have long.

Still, my stomach and chest continue to heave, and my body clings desperately to life, a reminder that it refuses to give up long after the mind has. Clawing my way along the smooth marble, I move toward the toilet, but once there, I am too tired to even lift my head.

I allow my eyes to close, and I say a silent prayer that whatever comes next, comes quick. I pray that my children never see me like this, that they never know how I suffered in the end. Then, I wait for the bright white light, but what I get instead is a knock at the bedroom door. It's soft at first and then more urgent. I hear a muffled voice, so familiar, followed by desperate pounding.

It doesn't matter. I can't open the door, even if I wanted to. I have no idea what killed me, but I sure as hell know who did.

CHAPTER ONE

Then

Ali

Seattle

He watches as she fastens her bra. His eyes never leave her as she searches for her panties, lingering as she slides them over her thighs. "Do you have to go?" David asks, solemnly.

She looks up and brushes the hair out of her eyes, only to have it fall back into place. Ali knows he loves it when she messes with her hair. He loves her optimism. He loves everything about her. "You know I do."

"Yeah." He flashes a smile. "But that doesn't mean I have to like it."

"This feels like guilt." She scans the room, looking for the items that she had laid out on the bed. Items that were supposed to have made it into her carry-on, but never did. Items that are now scattered on the floor. "We have a deal, remember?"

"Yeah, yeah. No guilt. No making you choose. I get it."

"Why do I sense a *but* coming?"

"There's no *but*," he says. "I just miss you when you're gone."

"And I miss you."

"I take it the session didn't go well."

Her brow raises just a hair and then her eyes soften. "What makes you say that?"

"I don't know," he shrugs. "How was the happy couple?" She hears the sarcasm in his voice. He doesn't know this, but she hates it when he follows a question with a question.

"You know I can't discuss that."

"Right, client privilege, of course. I was thinking...maybe it would be a good idea for you to stop seeing them."

"What?"

He sighs. "You're incredible, but I think you should work with people who at least have a shot."

"Who said they don't?"

He raises his chin slightly as his expression morphs from one of frustration to one of surprise. He runs his hand through his sandy blond hair, drops it to his side, and then stares at her with dark eyes. "I just assumed."

"You're too smart to make assumptions," she says, smiling mischievously, and leaves it at that. It's nice that she doesn't really have to talk about her work, or rather that she can talk about it without actually talking about it. The couple he is referring to paid triple her normal rate to have her fly to Seattle last minute, so his assumption is a fair one.

"While I'm digging myself into a hole...I think you work too hard."

He isn't wrong about that either. Not that she'll admit it. Therapy, sex therapy at that, particularly at the level she practices, is

KILL ME TOMORROW: A PSYCHOLOGICAL THRILLER

not a nine-to-five gig. "Unfortunately, relationship issues rarely follow a banker's schedule."

"So, you think they'll make it?"

"Define *make it?*"

"I don't know." His brow furrows. "You know...live happily ever after."

"No one lives happily ever after, my love." The truth is, no, she didn't think this couple will make it. However, admitting that would be a bit heavy for the moment, and he doesn't need to know any more than she wants him to. "It seems you've forgotten how good I am."

"Ah, yes. A momentary lapse. Perhaps I was hoping for a reminder."

"You just got one."

He strides over to her and takes her hand in his, intertwining their fingers, softening his approach. "You're right. I'm sorry." He pulls her toward him, pressing his body to hers. "Honestly—none of it matters. I'm just glad you came." *That's a half-truth*, she thinks, as he pulls away and searches her face. "And I really hate to see you go."

"So you've said." The way he looks at her brings back memories of what they just did. Him pinning her down, her pleasure muffled by the satin sheets. Skin on skin, sweaty and raw. One hand tangled in her hair, the other God knows where, pulling her under, silently pleading.

"I could cuff you to the bed."

Her eyes narrow. She could argue for her limitations. But she knows better. Ali knows if you argue for your limitations, you get to keep them. Obviously, she can't be in all places at once, but most limitations are more psychology than anything else. She could explain that she has clients, sessions that have been scheduled months in advance. She could tell him about the wait list that's a mile long. She could tell him how many years she's worked to get this far in her career. But what would be the point? "How about a rain check?"

A wry smile lights up his features, crinkling the corners of his eyes in a way that makes him seem older and wiser than he is. "Fine." He shakes his head. "Ball gag it is then."

She can't help but laugh as he grips the back of her neck, pulling her close once more. "Now you're talking." He's a pain in the ass, but the way he fucks makes up for it.

"It's not wrong to miss you," he whispers in her ear. "How can I help that I want more?" He releases the grip on her neck, steps back, and takes her in. "Who wouldn't?"

"You're right. It isn't wrong." She searches the floor for her discarded black pump. "Which is precisely why I'll be back on Tuesday."

He watches as she leans down and peers under the bed. The shoe could be anywhere in this mess. David goes borderline crazy whenever she leaves for a trip, and the bedroom reflects that. He gets restless and wild, demanding even. Not that she'd complain.

She pretends not to like the moods brought on by her absence, but secretly she wouldn't want it any other way. "There it is," she huffs, nearly breathless.

Her arm extends painfully as she strains to reach the missing shoe. Her fingers graze the tip and then slip. It's a stretch, but she fishes around until finally she makes contact and raises it triumphantly over her head.

"Damn," he says. "I was hoping you wouldn't find it. Hard to get to the airport barefoot."

"Not these days," she tells him, sliding backward before pushing up to a standing position. "They prefer you that way."

She turns around and freezes. A small gasp escapes her lips.

David, on bended knee, smiles up at her, his expression equally nervous and hopeful. Her eyes widen. It isn't like him, the nerves. He's as confident as they come.

In his palm rests a small velvet box. The lid is open. Next thing she knows, he's extending his arm upward, shoving a big shiny thing in her face.

She exhales slowly, and as she does, her face softens. Not because she's happy, although she can easily pretend, but because it came sooner than she expected. Although she's not entirely surprised, the disappointment is there nonetheless. There's something about men and their need to mark their territory, forever wanting to own her, that feels like a letdown.

"Sarah," he says, sucking in a deep breath. "I know it's only been a few weeks. I mean—believe me, I know this is crazy. But who cares? I want to spend the rest of my life with you, and I can't find any good reason to wait on getting started." He tilts his head ever so slightly as his brow lifts toward the ceiling. "Will you marry me?"

She feigns speechlessness, although there is much she ought to say. Her flight takes off in an hour. Better not chance it. She'd certainly miss her flight. "Yes!" she squeals. "Yes! Of course, I'll marry you!"

He stands and pulls her to him, squeezing so hard it knocks the breath out of her. "You have no idea. You've just made me the happiest man in the world."

He kisses her cheek first, and then her mouth, before trailing his lips along her collarbone. His lips are very effective. He's one of the good ones. The kind of man who makes it obvious he's had a lot of practice, the kind of man who likes to take his time. Which at the moment is a problem. She isn't dressed, and she's pressed for time. The perfect recipe for disaster.

"There will be other flights," he murmurs against her skin. "I'll make sure of it."

She doesn't argue because she understands. This is the way things are supposed to go. This is the way he sees it playing out in his mind. This is the way he's always envisioned it. This version is his fantasy, and some fantasies you don't disrupt. It's an invisible but important line, one she's learned needs careful towing.

He gently sucks at her neck, tracing an imaginary line down to the rounded curves of her breasts. He lingers. She breathes in the sandalwood scent of him as he relaxes into her.

"It's not fair that a woman should be this perfect." He glances up, his eyes meeting hers. He's confident, but like all men, he craves reassurance.

She could argue, as most women would. She could laugh him off, or find a reason to disparage herself, but she knows better. That's not her style. "So they say."

He laughs because it isn't a lie. It's obvious in the way other women look at her. Their expressions thinly veiled, it's easy to see what they are thinking. They're thinking it isn't fair. A woman with a small waist and large breasts has obviously had work done or starved herself. She hasn't and she doesn't. That's what she finds funny. Most women want to be thin. Most people want to be rich—talented, whatever—and yet, most people disparage those things when they see them.

Playfully, she pushes him back onto the bed. With his tanned skin and chiseled body, he could easily grace fitness magazine covers. He's not perfect, but he's pretty close. She reaches for the drawer beside the bed. It sticks, although with a bit of force, she slides it out. Shuffling blindly, she comes up with what she went in for. She holds the handcuffs in the air like an unspoken question, dangling them at eye level. "My turn."

"God," he sighs as she slips them around his wrists. "You never cease to—" She places her finger against his lips to silence him. He nips at it. "I love you, Sarah. I love you so much."

With a nod, she starts to offer a response, but can't decide where to start. It certainly isn't with the fact that her name isn't really Sarah.

CHAPTER TWO

Ethan

Austin

A chill settles over me as I scan the photographs for the umpteenth time. Looking for what, I don't know. Something I missed the first time? As many times as I've been over these images, I've yet to find anything inconsistent or out of the ordinary. Not that there is anything ordinary about looking at crime scene photos, but that's not the point.

The first photo is reminiscent of a sixteenth century painting. It shows a naked man in a seated position, one end of a rope looped around his neck, the other end fastened to a doorframe. His head hangs down and he's devoid of color, but otherwise he could just as easily have dozed off. Depending on one's definition of foul play, it doesn't give me much to go on. It's not a bad way to go out, if you ask me. I've seen worse.

A suicide according to the medical examiner's report, but my client refuses to believe that. There's an insurance payout for murder, and she's convinced her father's death was not intentional. Or more specifically, she said that it was no coincidence.

The second and third photos are pretty much the same, except they feature different men. Both men have slit wrists. The ME's report said they both had toxic amounts of cocaine in their systems, and neither left a suicide note.

The fourth image is the outlier. The only one technically classified as a murder. A naked male facedown on a bed, with a bullet wound in the back of his head. Simple. One and done.

There is nothing obvious connecting the four men, except they all had profiles on the same dating app. A connection it took an obscene amount of time to make. But then, that is what my client is paying me for. Although, after staring at images of naked men for hours on end, images I am not supposed to have and obtained using questionable methods, even though the fee my client is paying is substantial, it hardly feels like enough.

The familiar pang of acid building in my chest sets in. I reach into my desk and find only an empty bottle of antacids. I take this as a sign to set the pictures aside and call it a day. I'm interested, but not to the point of making any real headway. Maybe it's the weather. Maybe it's the heartburn. But whatever it is, it has me on edge. It's not just that I want to solve the case. That I *need* to solve the case. It's that other thing. Probably.

I take a few deep breaths in and hold them before slowly exhaling. I've been told this method is supposed to ease tension, but I have yet to feel it work. At any rate, my inability to focus isn't the end of the world. It's more likely the lack of sleep. Induced partially by the heartburn. A vicious cycle.

I know answers will come. Just not this minute.

Swiveling in my chair, I turn toward the window. Steady rain pelts the glass. Above, the sky hangs low with heavy gray clouds. Like most things, it won't last. The clouds will break within the hour, giving way to clear skies and bright sunshine, which reminds me I've always hated spring, so full of promise, most of them empty. Best-case scenario, it passes quick, and we break through to the dead heat of summer, to endless days and stifling heat. Otherwise, I might be tempted to crack the window and fling myself out. Not a bad way to go out either.

Below, the street is teeming with activity. Shrill horns and cars occupied by faceless people, commuters traveling back and forth on unchanging routes. I don't know how many minutes pass. I only know that I should be searching for a killer. Instead, the thought that ratchets back and forth in my mind is not how people have the strength to go on living this way, but how they have the strength to die here.

My assistant, Nadia, flings the door open, startling me. She slams a stack of papers down on my desk with a look of concern I know isn't real. "The info you requested."

I glance at the printed pages, which are not what I was expecting. I'd asked for this information three days ago and had since forgotten about it.

"I don't envy you," she says, her foot tapping to the beat of the rain outside. I wonder if she notices, but I doubt it. Nadia has a special brand of nervous energy she carries with her everywhere she goes, always has. Self-awareness is not her strong suit. She shakes her head. "Birthday parties aren't cheap."

"The price is the least of my concerns," I say, although that isn't entirely true. "It's screaming six-year-olds and their parents I could do without."

"Divorce sucks," she tells me. I've always liked that about her. Whatever's in that head of hers just comes tumbling right out of her mouth. It's refreshing, the clear-cut honesty.

"You know what sucks worse?"

"What?"

"Being in a miserable marriage."

She offers a hint of a smile. "I'll take your word for it."

Her lips press together as she appears to consider what she's about to say, whether she wants to dig her claws in or let it ride, although it's easy to see she's decided. "But Bethany is such a gem."

"I knew there was something that caused me to marry her." It was Bethany who'd hired Nadia. I never would have. She's become a permanent fixture in this tiny office, a reminder of what once was and isn't anymore. In hindsight, I should have seen her employment as a sign, the earliest sign that Bethany was slipping away. I hadn't. Nadia was a parting gift.

An interesting—if not fitting—gift, because Nadia is, to put it mildly, a younger, less angry version of my ex-wife.

Though I suspect that will change with time.

Nadia turns on her heel and flings her dark hair from her shoulder. Then she turns back, narrows her gaze, and lifts one brow toward the ceiling. "Tell me, what's changed?"

The way she says it all forceful-like makes me think she's testing me. Nadia is a very frustrated young woman, easily the type to go to Sex Addicts Anonymous just to pick up dates. Her contained rage serves the work we do here well. I'll give my ex-wife that much. Even if, in the end, the joke was on me. "What do you mean?"

"You were unhappy then," she shrugs. "You're unhappy now."

"I'm not unhappy."

She shrugs, offers her signature eye roll, and then struts toward the door. "If you say so."

"I say so," I call after her, but she doesn't look back. She closes the door, her nose turned upward, making it clear she's made her point and the conversation is over.

After she leaves, I sit and stare at the stack of papers she's left for a long time. I don't pick them up. Instead, I watch them closely as though they're a pit viper ready to strike. That's exactly what they are.

Planning a birthday party is not my forte, and that's putting it mildly. However, guilt is a powerful motivator and I've been warned, this is my year. I once thought I could get away from this type of demand with a divorce, but it's clear now that was wishful thinking at best, naive at worst.

To stall, I scan my email, checking various news sites. When that offers up nothing useful, I go back to staring out the window at the rain. In the end, no matter how many ways I find to procrastinate, the stack of papers remains. I know that sooner or later, someone will ask me about my progress, so I lift the documents and flip through the pages.

I find a huge list of everything from a petting zoo to pottery to rock climbing. There are basic packages, and, of course, the upgrades. I have no idea how one is supposed to choose. Or what the proper way to say "Happy birthday! I'm sorry your sister couldn't be here and it's my fault. I hope the balloons and the cake and the creepy clown make up for it" might be.

Whatever the case, the notion that I should handle this is absurd. I have a business to run and bills to pay. The simple solution would be to swallow my pride and let Nadia handle it. That's what I pay her for, and at least that way, when it goes wrong, I'll have someone to blame. Hell hath no fury like my ex-wife. But there's something in me that refuses to give in, something that understands I need to face the issue.

I set the party planning aside and turn back to the crime scene photos. I thought solving a murder was hard.

CHAPTER THREE

Ali

Flyover states

The flight is long, but she manages to catch up on work, putting the finishing touches on the talk she has scheduled tomorrow.

Even better, she met someone new. Andrew, hedge fund manager, youngish, single, and best of all, looking for something without strings. What a relief. Something she can work with.

She stretched out her legs to their full length. First class has its perks. David's treat, of course, since it was his fault she missed her previous flight. Ali fell in love with the look in his eye as he handed over his AmEx. Like it was nothing.

To him, it really is nothing. If David has trust issues, they've yet to show. Which is why she is glad she used a proper alias, one that she has proper documentation for. It could have gone very differently if she'd chosen not to dot her I's and cross her T's.

And yet, occasionally, the truth does come out. Not only does her work frequently put her in the public eye, Ali is self-aware enough to know that nothing stays secret forever. You can hide some things. But you can't hide everything. Thankfully, she has a solution and a straightforward answer if it comes to that. She's not *famous* famous or anything. Although, in her experience, even a little can go a long way. In the event she's caught red-handed, which has only happened once or twice, Ali has used it to her advantage, explaining that she wants to be known for *who* she is first and foremost and not for what she *does*.

How very wholesome. It can also be kind of sexy when framed the right way. People, men especially, eat that sort of thing up. Love is a cunning weaver of fantasies and fables.

Ali's ability to reinvent herself has allowed her to run her hustles. It has allowed her to live many lives. And she has. Which makes the first-class ticket a bit of a shame. She's always found that the interesting stories come from the people in the back. Sure, the legroom up front is nice. But, like most things, it comes with a price.

Thankfully, there's Andrew seated next to her. Andrew with his big eyes, expensive shoes, and endless tales of foreign lands. She appreciates the way he tries his hand at subtlety, even though it's obvious it's not the usual game he plays. There is something endearing about the way he glances at her laptop and smirks. When he finally catches her eye, he nods at her screen and the title of her talk: *Foreplay is f*cking fun.*

"And suddenly," he says. "I have so many questions."

She recognizes it immediately. His potential. It's too bad her plate is a little more than full at the moment.

As she laments over her jam-packed itinerary, she adds his info into her phone. Just in case. Ali is many things. Stupid isn't one of them. You never know when a little spare time might creep up, and there is that saying about idle hands. As she says in her work, life often has a way of surprising you.

CHAPTER FOUR

Ali

Boston

A car picked her up at the airport and dropped her downtown in front of her high-rise. As she steps out and into the perfect clear blue sky, she's reminded of why April is her favorite month of the year. Not only is the weather gorgeous, it's filled with hope and renewal. More than anything, she loves what a crapshoot the forecast is, how you never know what you're going to get. One second it can be calm with clear skies, and the next, at least here up North, you suddenly find yourself snowed in.

"I've missed that smile," the doorman says, greeting her with a playful bow.

"Oh, Melvin." She sweeps her long chestnut hair from her shoulder, sighing wistfully. "I bet you say that to all the girls."

He laughs and then shakes a pointed finger at her. "You got me."

As he lifts her bags from the trunk of the Town Car, he pauses and turns in her direction. "But none of them are as pretty as you, so this time it's the truth."

She offers him a wink and a smile. "I have no doubt."

Inside the building, as she presses the elevator button for the top, the six-carat diamond on her left hand catches her eye. She smiles as the elevator doors open and she steps in. During the ride, she thinks of Andrew from the flight. Andrew-with-the-potential, Andrew admiring her ring. She appreciates the not-so-honest honesty in his approach. He knows what she knows. If something without strings is what one is looking for, there's no better insurance policy than a giant rock on a woman's left ring finger.

"Hello," she calls, fumbling with the keycard, trying to remove it from the condo door. With one hand she struggles to hold the heavy door, with the other she drags her luggage over the threshold. "Anybody home?"

Edward wheels himself around the corner, a plate balanced on his right knee. His charcoal hair has grown while she was away. It hangs in his eyes, and she knows he hates when it gets that long. He's midbite as his brows rise. "Ali?"

"Were you expecting someone else?"

In one fell swoop, he tosses the plate onto the counter and pushes off, barreling toward her at full speed. He overshoots, clashing his chair against her left shin. She cries out. Edward leans forward and tries to help. He doesn't. "You're home early."

He takes her hand in his, lifts it to his mouth, and kisses it. The diamond has been replaced by the simple gold band he gave her three months ago. "My God I've missed you."

She sniffs the air. "You poor thing, what are you eating?"

28

"Leftover takeout."

"That's exactly what it smells like," she says, kicking off one black pump, and then the other.

He watches her as she walks over to the sofa and lifts the remote. She points it toward the floor to ceiling windows, pressing the button to open the shades. "It's nice out."

His expression shifts, and she knows he hasn't seen sunlight in days. He blinks his cerulean eyes several times, then shields them completely.

With a nod at his plate, she says, "I could cook for you."

"That's okay." It's remarkable. He looks like such a little boy when he lies. She can picture him as a child with his crooked smile, tousled hair, and skinned knees. "You must be beat."

"I slept on the flight."

He wheels over to where she stands in the middle of the open floor plan, slower this time. He stops in front of her, leans forward, and wraps his arms around the lower half of her body. It feels like a boa constrictor, snaking its way around her, and she wants to move away. But she doesn't. She won't. He burrows his face into her thighs. "I'm so glad you're home."

When he pulls away, he motions with one finger for her to turn around. She obliges and then knowing what he wants, more for reassurance than anything, she crouches down so he can unzip her dress. Painfully slowly, he slides it from her shoulders. "I've been waiting—"

She stands abruptly and wrinkles her nose. "I think I'll shower first. Airports are filthy places."

He grabs her wrist. His pale eyes flicker, seemingly turning several shades darker. "I can't wait any longer."

She knows he's lying, so she smiles and pushes off his chest. His eyes never leave her as she slinks toward the bedroom. He's had two infections in the last month alone. One that almost killed him. Not waiting is not an option. Aside from that, it's obvious he's let himself go while she was away. He reeks of onions and musty clothes. She doesn't know if she can bear it. Some things you can fake, others not so much. "I guess you'll have to join me then."

He does.

Later, after she's helped him dress and cooked something proper for him, she studies the way he scoots into bed. He's gotten so much better at transfers over the last few weeks. Much better than at the very beginning. She starts to tell him as much, but she knows he hates it when she points out the obvious. Their relationship cannot be sustained on pretension.

She held him in the shower as he sobbed, once again coming to terms that sex will not be the same. But she knows that was just one moment in time, one that needs to be carefully left where it was. Now stoicism is what he needs, so she flips out the light and climbs into bed beside him. They lay on their backs staring at the ceiling for a long time. Finally, he speaks, filling a void that neither is sure can ever truly be filled again. "I'm going back to work."

"What?" She props herself up on one elbow and looks over at him. She can just barely make out his features in the dark, and she can see that he's pleased at her surprise.

A half-smile appears across his face. "You heard me."

"You said you'd never go back."

"I had a meeting last week. With the partners."

"And?"

"And they said that if I was willing to give it a shot, they'd make accommodations."

"That's fantastic."

"I mean…" he sighs.

She can tell that whatever he's about to say, it doesn't come easily.

"Paraplegics work all the time. I don't see why I should be any different."

"Haven't I said that all along?"

"You were right," he says after another long sigh.

"What changed your mind?"

"Oh, I don't know…staring at these same four walls all the time. Your absence."

She senses there's more to it than that. "Anything else?"

"We lost one of my favorite patients last week."

"I'm so sorry, Edward."

"Me too. He hadn't even had a chance to live."

"How old?" she whispers, knowing he wants her to ask.

"Fourteen."

She doesn't know what to say, so she simply places her hand on his arm.

"I thought we had his case figured out. I thought we were in the clear."

"It's not your fault."

"No. But I should have been there." He shakes his head, his eyes meeting hers. "I wasn't though. I was here. Moping around feeling sorry for myself while children—children that I could have been working to save—were dying."

"I know how important your work is to you." She leans down and kisses his forehead. "It's the one thing I admire most about you."

Her hand trails down his face, then his chest, to his stomach, where she lingers before going lower. He won't feel her touch, but that isn't the point.

His face rests against her collarbone. "Thank God. You're my muse, Ali. You've always been my muse."

CHAPTER FIVE

I've always loved rooftops. So, naturally, this is where I take him. It's cold and clear out, making the night sky feel expansive and endless. If it weren't for the city lights, you could see stars for miles. The night is almost perfect, and still he cries.

"Show me," I say. Whatever it takes—anything to shut him up. But no. The whimpering goes on and on. It's quite pathetic in his half-hearted sort of way. "I said lie on the ground and show me."

Reluctantly, he complies. Sort of. He goes through the motions before he even hits the ground, but then he falters. Again, with the half-assing. "No," I said, making a clucking sound with my tongue. "Not like that. All the way."

He looks back over his shoulder and meets my eye, even though he's been warned not to do it again. "It's freezing out."

"You won't feel it if you're dead."

I see it then, the flash in his eyes as he weighs his options. Same as they all do. He thinks he can overpower me, and perhaps he's right.

Thankfully, we won't have to find out because I brandish my gun.

The great equalizer.

"Fine," he stutters. "Yes. Okay." His knees shake as he lowers himself down.

"Now show me."

He rests his cheek against the reinforced concrete and simulates sex. Then he peeks over his shoulder. "Was that good?"

"Get up," I hiss. "And don't look at me again."

I order him to face outward. Toward the buildings, toward the night.

Next thing I know, he throws himself over the ledge and plunges headfirst seven stories to the ground. I close my eyes, and turn my back, but I can't close my ears to the sickening *whomp* of his body smashing against the pavement, the sound of his bones snapping and shattering.

I don't mean to look down. But I can never quite refuse myself the opportunity, not after so much hard work. His body lies in the street just short of the curb, spread-eagle and faceup.

From this high up, his face is featureless, but even at street level, I gather that all the bones in his body have been pulverized. Blood will have begun pooling around his head, dampening the hair plugs he spent a small fortune on.

A small crowd quickly grows around him. A smattering of strangers, people whose night and perhaps beyond, he will have ruined, just the same as he did mine. Good riddance, I say.

As for the onlookers, they stare down at him, and then point upward toward the sky, toward where I am standing, and while I know they can't see me at this angle in the dark, I also know I'd better get a move on.

CHAPTER SIX

Ethan

Austin

There are a thousand ways to die, and as I sit in traffic on Loop One, I contemplate them all. *Get eaten by a bear?*

Nah. Too painful. Not quick enough. Bears are omnivores. The way they eat humans does not differ from the way they eat berries from a branch. They'll rip your limbs off one by one and chew you to death while you're still alive.

That very much sums up what my life has been like over the past eighteen months. But we'll get to that.

Get caught in a mudslide?

I glance around. The chances of a mudslide in Austin traffic are slim. The rain has passed. There's no mud. Just an endless sea of taillights. Up ahead, someone else's mistake, someone else's impatience, someone else's inattention in the form of a fender bender is costing me an hour of my life. Horns sound as vehicles attempt to maneuver from one lane to another. Monkey see. Monkey do. Whether it's the right move is anyone's guess. God, I long to leave the city. I hate traffic. I hate confined spaces. I hate people.

Go down in quicksand?

Been there, done that. Bethany couldn't see herself living anywhere else. Austin has always been home for her. It turns out you can't take Texas out of the girl, or the girl out of Texas. And now, with the kids in school, and the fact that we share custody makes it hard for me to leave.

At nine and nearly six, I can't say the divorce has been any kinder to my kids than it has been to me. Kelsey has withdrawn into herself while Nick acts out. Not that I've seen any of these behaviors myself, but the family therapy appointment in forty-five minutes is where my ex-wife and a court order assure me they will both get sorted out.

Suffocation.

The judge's ruling is the only reason I go along with it, much less pay for it. I don't have a choice. The divorce wasn't my idea, although I wasn't against it. Especially not after Bethany announced she was in love with another woman. That was the first blow, followed by the jarring realization that she'd rather be in *that* relationship than remain a family.

I can't say her proclamation blindsided me, but I can't say it hadn't either. A wife who likes other women may sound like any man's wet dream, but they haven't met my ex-wife's new girlfriend.

Sepsis.

Finally, I pass the accident, and traffic begins to flow. It's almost disappointing how minor the accident is, considering how much time it has set me back. Anticlimactic, and yet it feels like a decent metaphor for my life. If you're not careful, your choices will get you stuck.

Choking causes thousands of deaths each year.

If I'm late to therapy I risk losing shared custody, and since I have no idea how I'd explain that to my children, I shift the car into gear and gun it. Bethany despises me enough these days as it is, and I have every suspicion she doesn't hold back in letting our kids know what a fuck-up their father is. I do what I can not to give her any added ammunition.

A dream that is short-lived when I see the flashing lights behind me.

Suicide by cop?

I take the first exit I come to and drive a little ways, before I find an empty lot. I make a right turn into the parking lot and come to a complete stop. I watch in the rearview mirror as the officer pulls in behind me.

Following a rather impressive strut from his car to mine, the officer shimmies up to my driver's side window and peers in. His shades teeter precariously on the tip of his nose, although it's nearly dark. He seems familiar, and then I realize why.

He's a doppelgänger for Ponch from the TV show CHiPs. He's as bad a knockoff as I've ever seen. Maybe it's because trying so hard. It's too much. I start laughing. It comes in spurts at first, and then I can't help myself. I can't breathe.

His stern look and the shake of his head force me to muffle my laughter. He has really nice hair. "I clocked you doing eighty-eight in a sixty-five."

I'm almost sure it was faster than that, but I won't argue. I could confess that I'm trying to get to therapy, but with swagger like that, I know it won't matter. "That's why I bought this car."

"Ah. A wise guy," he says, adjusting his shades. "Just my luck."

I take it that means I'm not getting off with a warning, and I watch as he removes a Maglite from his hip and shines it inside the vehicle. Finally, he meets me eye to eye. "License and registration, please."

"I'm a CHL holder," I say, handing over my license.

His eyes narrow. I can tell this is more than he bargained for as well. "Step out of the car, please."

He asks me where the firearm is located and when I say it's on my person; he asks me to remove it and hand it to him. This being the most complicated and least desirable option he could have suggested, I tell him I'm going to unbutton my shirt and let him retrieve it from the holster himself.

His method, while a serendipitous offer, one that could get me out of family therapy indefinitely, would be an easy way to die. Easier than I thought. But death at the hands of a Ponch lookalike seems a tad dramatic, even for me.

He takes the firearm and places it in his cruiser, and then issues me a ticket. Once he's painstakingly and methodically gone through all the motions in a manner designed to guarantee that I'm as late as possible, he hands my weapon back and gives me permission to be on my way.

"Excuse me," I call out, leaning out my window just as he's about reached his cruiser. If he's going to issue me a ticket, the least he can do is give me some goddamned stickers for the kids.

CHAPTER SEVEN

Ali

Austin

Ali's exhausted after her workshop, but in the best way. It's that high-level euphoria type of tired she is so familiar with whenever she knocks it out of the park, which she definitely did this evening.

There's nothing quite like watching a group of women, along with a dozen or so enlightened men, walk away satisfied. And if they weren't, well, they would be soon.

Foreplay is f*king fun is one of her favorite and best attended talks. After all, knowledge is power—and power is sexy. This particular workshop aligns very well with what she teaches of the Kama Sutra.

When the Kama Sutra offers advice on how to be a "desirable

woman," it suggests that before marriage women should learn "all the required forms of art," ranging from reading about worldly affairs to playing an instrument or knowing how to make a bed. And, of course, a desirable woman should study the sixty-four sexual positions that the Kama Sutra is known for. Despite it sounding terribly old-fashioned, Ali agrees with the idea that a well-rounded person is more attractive. Her personal motto: Doing squats is great, but so is reading.

To celebrate the end of a successful workday, she does what she often does. She lets her hair down. She practices what she preaches. Tonight, she is practicing at The Roosevelt Room.

Set in a building built in 1929, it's one of her favorite bars in the city. She appreciates the classic design and modern touches and how the two blend perfectly, coming together in a beautiful and tasteful way.

Across the dining room, she can feel his eyes on her. Written on his face is this thought: *Is it you?*

The back and forth between them is a dance, candlelit, and also his choice. Briefly, she makes eye contact. A shy smile before she looks away, her eyes scanning the room, as though she too is looking for something she hasn't already found and perhaps she is.

As for him, she knows he's expecting a redhead. Someone mousy, quietly attractive. Someone with potential. Definitely not her.

He frowns slightly. Ali bets he's thinking that his mind is playing tricks on him. There's a familiarity about her, but she is not *her*. Or is she? *Could she be?* Could he be that goddamned lucky? Just this once. Could this be the opposite of the profile pic bait and switch? Instead of someone ten years and twenty pounds heavier, could things ever go the opposite way?

They can, Stan, she thinks. With a bit of effort.

No, he decides finally. She can see his decision in the twist of his mouth. Stan Reynolds does not believe he is that lucky. What a shame. He smiles and nods his head before turning back to the bar. It's not a quick brush-off. His eyes linger, so he is not completely deterred. He's meeting a woman, but he is not married to her, and if something better were to come along, he would not discount the opportunity.

Ali smiles back because this game they are playing is fun. After the week she's had, she's in the mood for a bit of that, and she likes that he does not shy away.

Her phone pings, a notification from the app, a new message. It's one of hundreds she receives in a day. On a busy day, that is, and still usually no fewer than fifty on a slow one. This happens when you're reasonably attractive and a professional. It helps for sure if you say you aren't looking for anything serious, which is not a lie. She isn't. It's important to be honest, at least about the things that matter.

Ali is smart. People pick up on the big lies. The little ones, like the color of your hair, or your interests, those are interchangeable and can be easily manipulated. Her work has taught her many things, one of them being that people are naturally suspicious. Something she's learned to use to her advantage.

She walks across the crowded restaurant, toward the bar where Stan is seated. The barstool next to him is empty, and she wonders briefly if he's been saving it, or if it is mere luck, but in the end, she knows it doesn't matter. A chance encounter that isn't chance at all.

He looks down at his phone, although he is very much aware of her presence. He's not intentionally ignoring her. He's conflicted. The smart move would be to ask her to take the seat, strike up a conversation, make himself seem desirable, so that when the woman he is actually expecting shows up, he has a leg up.

But Stan here isn't much of a forward thinker. He isn't thinking about that. Ali knows he's thinking about sex and the easiest way in which he might get it. He isn't thinking long term, and that is exactly where she wants him.

When the bartender comes over, she orders her usual, a martini. Dirty. There's a jazz band playing, and she too glances at her phone before placing it in her clutch. Then she swivels in her chair to face the band. Slowly, she sips her martini. And she waits.

Stan dips his fingers in the peanut bowl and shoves a few in his mouth. This tells her a lot about him, about what he's like in bed. Careless. Confident. An interesting combination. She knows it's odd that one could determine this much about a person based on a simple dip into a snack bowl, but she's watched a lot of people. And of course, there's his dating profile, chock full of information about all the other facets of his life.

He's into rugby, and was married once, briefly. Never wants to do that again and who can blame him? The ex made out well, leaving poor Stan with the legal bills, a ton of insecurity, and a fair amount of disenchantment. That's okay though. What has been torn down can easily be rebuilt.

"Can I get you another?" the bartender asks Stan. She glances over her shoulder at him, interested in his answer. He checks the time on his watch. A Rolex. Engraved on the bottom. It was a wedding gift from his ex, according to the life events on his Face-book page. Ali wonders why he still wears it, but she understands it's not so much nostalgia as it is that Stan is the practical type and that makes her smile a little. A challenge. "I don't think so. If she's this late, it's usually a sign."

"There was an accident on Loop One," she interjects. "Took me forever to get through."

"She could have texted," Stan says.

"Texting and driving is dangerous."

"She could have called."

"Still dangerous."

He considers her. She's not only piqued his interest visually, but intellectually. "Sure," he says to the bartender, who is not nearly as taken with her, not for holding him up. "Might as well. I'll take one more."

"Better to have the glass half full," she says, fingering the stem of her martini glass.

"And you," he says. "Are you waiting for someone?"

He's forward and she appreciates that. "Me? No. I'm here for the band."

"Oh, yeah?" He points to the man playing bass. "That guy there —he's my college roommate."

So he is a bit of a forward thinker. Smart move. He suggested they meet at a place he's familiar with, where he knows someone. She smiles, but she's not surprised. It's difficult to get to Stan's level of wealth without a bit of intelligence. "You'll have to introduce me."

He nods. It's an invitation but not an obvious one. It's a challenge.

"You should text her."

He looks over at her, confused.

"The woman you're waiting on."

"Oh. Right."

Her brows raise. "But didn't you just say it was dangerous?"

"For her. Not for you."

He doesn't follow. Stan is not conscientious. With his intelligence, wealth, and moderate good looks, attentiveness is something he's gotten by without. She often finds the higher a man's net worth, the lower they fall on the mindful scale.

"Make sure everything is okay."

He waves her off and takes a long sip of his tequila. "People are so flaky these days. I'm not surprised."

"Blind date?"

"You could say that."

She shifts in her seat. "Would you like to dance? I feel like dancing."

Stan tilts his head. "Here?"

"Unless you know somewhere else."

He scans the room. "There's no dance floor."

"Semantics," she says, hopping off the stool. She holds out her hand.

Reluctantly, Stan takes it.

CHAPTER EIGHT

One second he's completely satisfied, smug even, and the next his face is twisted in agony.

One thing is for sure. He isn't expecting to see me there. This is obvious by the surprise on his face. But then there's more, there's something else. A friendly ease, perhaps. Like most people, he doesn't immediately see me for what I am. Or rather, *who* I am.

"Well, hello," he says, a sly smile sliding across his face.

"Hello, Stan."

I move toward him. "I was hoping you could help me with something."

"Sure," he nods. He's confused, but he's too polite to show it. "Anything."

As he waits for me to state my favor, he offers another smile, this one different, tighter, less sure, one that he doesn't know— that he can't know—will be his last.

From that point, everything goes fast. How he ends up tied to his bed, his wrists slit with a hefty amount of cocaine in his system, it's all a blur. Both to him and me.

CHAPTER NINE

Ethan

"Tell us about the bad guy, Daddy."

I glance in the rearview mirror. "How's school going?"

"Fine," they shout in unison.

"Now, tell us."

It's inevitable, this conversation, and I'm prepared. It's a reoccurring line of questioning anytime we're in the car together, which at this stage of life seems to be a lot. They want to know about the perp I am trying to catch. They want details on the case, or cases, I am working on.

More often than not, I offer them a made-up version, sometimes, but not always with a sliver of the truth. This allows me to insert my message, usually as a life lesson, into the cracks. *Don't talk to strangers. Stay away from dark alleys. Keep your friends close, enemies closer.* That sort of thing.

On one hand, I'm glad they're interested in my work as a private investigator. On the other, they're getting to the age where my omissions are becoming more and more apparent. Not that this is inherently bad. I want them to ask good questions. I want them to understand when they're being deceived. At the same time, I'm not sure I'm ready yet to let them know just what a scary place this world can be. Innocence is a beautiful thing, a thing that, once taken, cannot be handed back. And they've had enough taken as it is.

"Dad!" Kelsey screeches. "You promised."

"Dad." I feel Nick's eyes burning holes in my back. "You did say."

"Okay, okay, fine. Well, it's not a bad *guy*. It's a bad *girl*. At least that's what the police suspect."

"Girls can't be bad," Kelsey says, her nose scrunched, eyes narrowed.

"Pffft," Nick scoffs.

"I mean they can't kill anyone." The way she says it, I can tell exactly the point, somewhere around midsentence, where she starts to question her own logic.

"You're such a child," Nick says.

"They can't! Right, Daddy?"

"Tell her," Nick insists.

"Darling, I assure you, they can."

"Is that what Uncle Max said?" Nick inquires. "That it was a woman?"

"He suspects it is, yes. But he doesn't know for sure. That's why he asked me to help." This isn't entirely true. Max is not actually my brother, and he didn't ask for my help. Max works for the police department. As a favor and because he's my friend, he feeds me information. Leaking crime scene photos and information central to an investigation is not only unethical, it's illegal. But if it catches a murderer before he or she kills again, does it matter?

Probably. But that's a problem for another day.

The chatter settles and the questions fade as I pull into the parking lot of their favorite pizza place. Every Wednesday is my night, according to the most recent court order. After the therapy session, we come here to Pike's to unwind and to enjoy the combination of mediocre pizza and overpriced arcade games.

They could never get their mother in a place like this, so it's a treat for all of us. Not to sound bitter. I may not like Bethany, but there's a part of me that still loves her. Beth's the type of person who's easy not to like, but hard to hate. It doesn't help that I see her for exactly who she is, the way one does when love and shared history erases the rest.

People contain a multitude of layers, and while my ex-wife may put up a hard front, deep down there's more to it than that. Bethany is not a bad person, she's just broken.

If she were going to move on and split our family in two, I would have preferred that she were at least happy about it. And that's the crux. I don't know what she thought she'd find—greener grass, perhaps—but clearly that is not the reality. That's why she hates me so much, and that's why she continues to blame me even though her life is the result of the choices she made. Except, of course, for the one thing, which was my fault, and it unraveled everything.

AFTER I ORDER THE PIZZAS, THE KIDS GRAB A TABLE, AND I FEED dollars into the change machine. As my plastic cup fills with coins, the therapy session replays in my mind.

Once the children had been sent out into the waiting room to work on homework, I was met with a combined look of pity and disdain on the women's faces. Bethany started in with her hemming and hawing immediately, and the therapist followed right along. The sound of disbelief was obvious in her voice, and the rigid set of her shoulders made her feelings known. It mattered not that I'd explained the situation forward and backward. That I hadn't meant to be late had little effect.

Apparently, a traffic citation is not the same thing as a get out of jail free card nor did it work to my advantage. Instead of making it appear that I truly cared and hence drove like a bat out of hell to make the appointment on time, my tardiness had the opposite effect, making me appear reckless and ostentatious. This is why I will never understand women.

"You always did lose track of time," Bethany remarked. "But this time is different, Ethan. As far as I'm concerned, this is the final straw." She paused to look at the therapist for comfort or approval. "The kids were depending on you to be here. And once again you've let them down. You've let us all down."

"I can't control traffic."

"Come on," Beth huffed. "This isn't about traffic and you know it."

"What is it about?" the therapist asked, glancing from me to Bethany and back.

"It's about the fact that he can't move on and he's punishing me."

"That's not true," I lied.

"Prove it," Bethany said.

The therapist eyed me as she shifted in her chair, easing in, readying herself to pounce. "Would you say you're moving on, Mr. Lane?"

I have no idea why I said what I said next. Maybe it was the fact that they were coming at me like a firing squad. I only know that the words just rolled off my tongue. "I'm seeing someone."

The look on my ex-wife's face alone was almost worth the price of the lie. Whatever that turns out to be.

Bethany's head whipped around. "Since when?"

"I don't know." I shrugged. "Does it matter?"

For the first time in a long time, I was met with silence.

"This is good," the therapist remarked. "This is progress."

"It's not serious," I said.

"But you're dating," the woman replied gently. "That's a good first step."

I cocked my head proudly. "Is it?"

Bethany stared at her hands. As usual, it was impossible to tell what she was thinking. Eventually, tears welled in her eyes. "I'm so glad, Ethan." She drew in a deep breath and then let it out slowly. "This has been so hard—"

She has no idea.

"Tell him how you feel," the therapist pressed.

"What I mean is—I thought you were never going to get over me. You don't know what a relief this is, or how much guilt I've carried around."

Typical Bethany. Ever the narcissist. High on drama. She positively glowed when everything was about her.

"It has nothing to do with you," I said, leaning back in my seat. "I was just waiting for the right person to come along. Like you did."

"DAD!" KELSEY SCREECHES. "NOW CAN WE?"

My mind flits back to the present, to the coins overflowing the cup, spilling over the side, dropping onto the floor. "Now can you what?"

Nick is already collecting coins, keeping an eye out for anyone who might dare encroach.

His sister could not care less. She tugs at my shirt. "Now can we go play?"

"You said we could play games first tonight," Nick says, shoving a fistful of tokens in his pocket.

My daughter looks at me expectantly. "Yeah! You promised!"

"That I did." I hand the cup to Nick. "Split this with your sister."

Kelsey beams. "We can go?"

With a nod, I pat my son on the back. "Be sure to subtract what you've already stuffed in your pocket."

Once they're successfully immersed in side-by-side games of pinball, I locate an empty booth by the exit and move the drinks from the table they chose to one that gives me a three-hundred-and-sixty-degree view of the place. Then I take out my phone and tap the dating app. *Beacon.*

The idea came in traffic and solidified itself in the midst of the therapy session. If my client is right, and her father was murdered, I realize if I'm going to catch the killer, I have to think like one. Sometimes the simplest answers are the most obvious ones.

I also think of my ex-wife and how it's better not to be a liar.

CHAPTER TEN

Ethan

When I request she see me in my office, Nadia feigns a headache. I offer her two aspirin and the corner seat. I have to buzz her three times, but eventually she comes sulking in and slinks down into the chair. She rubs at her temples, while giving me the death stare. "We got another call from Spectrum," she says, dropping her hands into her lap. "They're going to shut us off if we can't pay them half by Monday."

"Great. Okay. I'll figure it out." I jot a note down on the notepad beside me: *Call the internet company.* Then I meet Nadia's eyes. "But that's not why I called you in here."

She blows her bangs away from her face and juts out her bottom lip. "You're laying me off."

"Of course not. Why would you think such a thing?"

"You can't even afford the internet," she says, shrugging.

She has a point, which I ignore by scooting back from my desk and kicking my feet up on it. I lean back in my chair and cradle the back of my head in my palms. "Let me ask you something, Nadia. How do you meet men?"

She glares at me with a sly grin. "I don't think this is workplace conversation. Are you itching to get sued?"

Been there, done that. But that's a topic for another time, which is probably never. "What do you know about creating a dating profile?"

She relaxes into the chair. Her interest is piqued. "Well, that depends. Are you desperate to get laid or are you trying to catch a killer?"

"The latter, definitely."

"Oh. In that case—" she starts, pausing as a mischievous look passes across her face. "Why not just copy the profiles of the victims? Perhaps our killer has a type. Most of us do."

"Right. That's what I was thinking," I lie, realizing that after nearly half a century I still have so much to learn about women. Ninety-nine percent of the time, nothing they do or say makes any sense. Even as I searched for commonalities between the victims, Nadia's suggestion hadn't crossed my mind. Who wants to date the same person over and over? But then glancing up I remember that my assistant is a carbon copy of my ex-wife, and things make a bit more sense.

I swivel my computer monitor around so that Nadia can see the screen. She stands, comes over to my side of the desk, and flips the screen back around. "You know I hate to strain my eyes," she says, leaning over me.

It's the same distance, I almost say, but I don't waste my breath.

She rests her elbows on top of my desk and sprawls out. "Better."

She squints as she reads. When she's finished, she sighs and stretches out, her lanky frame further invading my space. I wait for her to say something but instead she rubs at her temples. I can tell she isn't impressed with what I've written. Nadia is not one to hide her emotions well.

"That's just what I have so far."

She glances at the computer and then back at me before breaking into hysterical laughter.

"It's not that bad," I say. "I've seen worse."

"Wait," she chokes. She pushes off the desk and holds one finger up. "It's just—" She tries to get the rest of the sentence out, but she can't contain her laughter. Her pale skin flushes, and soon her face and neck have broken out in red splotches. "I can't believe *you* got accepted on Beacon."

"Well, I did."

"With a bio like that?" Her eyes widen. "Wow."

"What is that supposed to mean?"

"It screams middle-aged dad."

"It doesn't say that. I don't mention my kids anywhere."

"You don't have to. It's in the context."

As usual, I have no idea what she's talking about.

Again, she's consumed with laughter. "I'm sorry," she snorts. "I just can't get over the fact that they let you in."

"I don't understand."

"I have friends who've been waiting for months! Friends that were denied. You know, actual cool people." She shakes her head. "Fucking algorithms."

"You said that."

"Well, Beacon is—" she recovers long enough to catch her breath. "It's a very exclusive app. Honestly, they don't let just *anyone* in."

"I'm not just anyone."

"Yeah, sure, Mr. FBI. I know. I've heard the stories."

"*Former* FBI. Professional liar is more accurate these days. P.I. work is not glamorous, if you couldn't tell."

She turns toward the window. "You must miss it."

"Not really."

When she meets my eye again, she knows she's pressed a raw wound, and she softens, or at least as much as possible for a woman like Nadia. "You should put your height in there. Women love that."

"I doubt the suspect cares."

"The dead men in that stack of photos tell a different story."

"Okay, I'll add my height to my bio."

"Give yourself the liberty of adding an inch or two. It's not like anyone's going to show up with a measuring tape."

This time it's me who laughs. She doesn't know women the way she thinks she does. "You never know."

I wait for her to speak, but when it looks like she has nothing else to add to the conversation, I rub my palms together. "What else?"

She studies me for a long moment. "You don't date much, do you?"

"I do all right."

"Well, if you've been on a dating site or app for any time at all, you've probably noticed that most profiles look very similar to one another." Her brow arches. "It's like everyone is playing some bland game of Mad Libs. You just fill in the blanks of the same exact profile. 'Hi, I'm blah! I have these three good traits and an ideal virtue you wish you had but don't. I enjoy [activity] with my friends or watching [popular television show or movie] at home. I'm here to [hedge and say you want to meet new people], and I'd love to [flirtatious invitation].'"

"Yeah, well, I don't have friends and there aren't many activities I enjoy."

She shifts her stance. "C'mon, boss, that's my point. You're more than the sum of your Netflix queue! Where's the originality? Where's the panache? Dating profiles shouldn't read like job resumes. Your personality, sense of humor, and storytelling ability are far more important than straight facts and demographics. It's an art. You have to draw people in."

"Great. But I still don't know what that means. And stop calling me boss."

"Whatever. Let's take another look at the profiles of the dead guys."

"The victims."

"Whatever." She gets a look on her face whenever she concentrates. All business. Pure logic. Low emotion. "First thing you have to consider is that the average reply rate is only about 30 to 50 percent for men. So what you want to ask yourself is what they all had in common. How did they get her attention—much less a date?"

"That's exactly what I've been doing. For weeks."

"Here Donovan Roberts." She grabs the mouse, reinvading my personal space. She clicks on his file, and then drags the folder that contains the crime scene photos across the desk, hitting my cold cup of coffee in the process. I grab the mug before it topples over. Nadia points at the screen. "Says here he likes live music and travel."

"Everyone likes that."

"Yes, but if you notice, he wrote that he wasn't looking for anything serious. He's living in the here and now. At least he was, anyway. He wasn't talking about the future. And neither was Michael Hollis or Kevin Stewart or Stan Reynolds. Their profiles specifically state they were looking to network," she says, using air quotes for "looking to network". "They were interested in making professional connections, whereas what you have here suggests you're up for walking down the aisle next month."

"Isn't that what women want?"

"Apparently not this woman. And even if it were, most women on dating sites aren't going to admit that."

"Right, not until the second date. At least."

"Maybe you don't know women the way you think you do, boss."

"Maybe not. But this all sounds like a lot of wasted time."

"It's not wasted time. It's a game—and a numbers game at that."

"Games are for children."

"Don't worry." She winks. "Even if you say you're in it for the 'professional connections,' there's still a good chance of getting laid."

CHAPTER ELEVEN

Ethan

Nadia deftly rewrote my bio. A few keystrokes and she assured me it was not only perfect, but also ripe with opportunity. According to my profile, I'm an attorney, age forty-five to fifty, height six-foot-two, who likes live music, has traveled to seventy-eight countries, speaks four languages, and competes in triathlons in my spare time. I also happen to volunteer at my local animal shelter and hope to expand my circle through "networking."

So, basically, I sound like every other man on these sites. If you live in fantasyland, that is, which apparently most women do.

To say I'm out of practice would be an understatement. Dating should be easy enough. I'm no stranger to asking questions, to gathering information and making a determination. In my work, I base most decisions on gut feelings, using my intuition. But a date isn't the same thing. It's not supposed to go down like an interrogation. Or that's exactly what it's like. It's just not supposed to feel like it.

Online dating is not so different. I'm only telling a story. I'm playing a part, same as all the other cases in my old life with the FBI. Before I was an analyst, I started out working undercover.

Online, with my dating profile, I'm a made-up person, and like all good actors, I'm playing a version of myself, different and yet similar enough to make it believable.

For the sake of efficiency, and the fact that I have children plus a company to run, I've handed over my communication on Beacon to Nadia who does a phenomenal job pretending to be me, a man looking to meet women. Her replies and back-and-forth banter are impressive. Thanks to her, my reply rate is easily 60 percent and creeping upward by the day. Even so, I set the cap at three dates. By then, I'll know whether this might work or whether I'm wasting my time, and with any luck, a little more about how the killer thinks.

Nadia sets the dates up at a wine bar about ten blocks from the office, scheduling them an hour and a half apart. That leaves thirty minutes between each encounter, and she made it clear to my dates that I have an appointment with a client in half an hour, meaning that I am pressed for time. I will go so far as to exit the bar, so as not to run over time or get stuck with stragglers.

The first woman is attractive, in her midforties. She arrives fifteen minutes late, something I forgive, because she blames traffic, and also there's the attractive part. She downs three glasses of pinot noir in fifteen minutes while talking non-stop, mostly about her ferrets. "I'm new in town," she says. "You?"

"Ah, yeah. Well, kind of."

"Where do you stay?"

"Stay?"

"You know, live? Where do you live?"

"Oh. North," I lie.

"No way! Me too." She shifts in her chair and then leans in.

"Well, I'm staying with friends. But I'm looking to put down roots."

I nod and she goes on. "I really appreciate the art scene here. I mean, Austin is great for that. Especially for someone like me."

"Someone like you?" I practice mirroring, a psychology technique which is really just repeating back portions of what the other person said, in the form of a question.

"Yeah. I'm trying to break into performance poetry."

"Never heard of it."

"Poetry."

"No, poetry I've heard of. The latter."

"Oh," she waves her hand in the air. "You'll have to come see me perform."

"Sure."

"Listen, I don't want to beat around the bush. I don't sleep with men on the first date."

"Yeah, me either."

"Ha," she says draining her drink. "You're funny."

"Am I?"

"Yeah. Anyway, no sex. But blowjobs aren't out of the question."

I choke on my own spit and signal the server for the check. "I'm sorry," I say. "I have to go feed my cat."

"I love cats!"

"You'd hate this one. He's evil."

Her face falls. "Ah." She points her index finger at me. "I see what you're doing. You're brushing me off."

"Nah."

"You know what?" She stands abruptly, nearly knocking the chair over in the process. "Fuck you! I didn't even like you anyway!"

THE SECOND WOMAN, ROSE, ARRIVES SEVEN MINUTES EARLY AND was probably attractive once upon a time. Instead of being forty-six as she listed on her profile, I'd put her in the range of seventy-six and then some. I've always been a fan of older women, but this is a stretch.

"So you're an accountant," she asks.

"Unfortunately."

"I'm a widow," Rose says in a manner that tells me she was looking for any means possible to insert that fact into the conversation.

"I'm sorry."

"Me too." She offers a sad smile. "It's horrible losing a spouse, let me tell you. Have you ever been married?"

"Me?" I shake my head. "No."

"That's too bad." She glances around the place. "This isn't my typical scene."

I'd bet not.

She looks back at me and smiles. "But I can be flexible. Now that I'm retired, especially. In fact, what I'm looking for is a travel companion." She lowers her chin. Her eyes search mine. "Do you like to travel, Mark?"

I don't know how to break it to her that I have school-age children or that she's older than my mother. "Me? No. I hate anything new. I hate flying."

"What about trains?"

"Especially trains. I get motion sickness."

"Huh," she says like she doesn't buy it.

"Really, I'm a routine kinda guy."

"Funny," she tells me. Her brow knits and she shakes her head. "That's not what your profile says."

"I'm a liar. Pathological."

Her eyes widen. "That sounds like a problem."

"Believe me, it is."

She leans away and then crosses her arms over her chest.

"The truth is, my bio is just a front. What I'm really looking for is a one-night stand."

Rose lets her hands fall into her lap. She stares at them. "Normally. I hate liars," she says, glancing up at me. "But like I said, I can be flexible."

I signal the server to close out the tab.

Rose holds her hands up, palms facing me. "You don't have to be in such a rush."

I wonder if she heard what I said about one-night stands and judging by the smile on her face, I'm afraid she did. "You never know," she says. "This evening could lead to more."

THE THIRD WOMAN, CALLIE, IS PUSHING *MAYBE* TWENTY-ONE. IN fact, I'm not confident she isn't actually jailbait. I don't know what it is about women and lying about numbers, but here we are. When I ask why she lied, she says it's a bad habit, the way one might chew with their mouth open or leave the lights on when they exit a room.

"What can I say," she smacks. She's chewing a wad of gum like it's going out of style. "I like older men."

"That's obvious." I consider the ages of the victims. "What else do you hate?"

"Oh," she says, rolling her eyes from side to side. The chewing never stops. "You know, anything traditional, work included."

"Work included?"

"Well, I do have six hundred thousand Instalook followers."

"Impressive."

"Right? I like to think of myself as an influencer, but brand deals were slow this year." She speaks in a pouty voice, that makes me want to find the nearest fork and stab my eardrums until I can no longer hear.

"It's okay though," she continues. "It's turned out to be a good thing." She pauses long enough to fidget with her hair. It's almost like the talking and the chewing and the twisting a strand around her finger is too much to do all at once. "A really good thing, actually! It's given me more time to focus on meeting interesting people face-to-face. Like you!"

"That is interesting."

The server arrives. Callie orders a margarita on the rocks, and she gets carded. The female server gives me the stink eye. "We're networking," I say, and I wouldn't be surprised if she didn't spit in my drink.

After "barely legal" leaves, Nadia shoots me a text. *Stay put. Something just came through. She is right around the corner and is up for meeting you.*

I said three dates. So I text back the best one-word answer in the entire English language: *no.* I'm exhausted. On average, women speak about twenty thousand words per day to a man's seven thousand. I'm easily upwards of ten.

Nadia responds, telling me she has a feeling about this one. Then she asks if I called the internet company, a not-so-subtle reminder that I need to solve this case. God, I hope that whoever this woman is, she can carry the conversation. *Send me her profile,* I write back.

MY PHONE VIBRATES. FINALLY, A REPLY FROM NADIA. *SOME investigator you are, just pull up the app. BOLO for a woman with red hair and green eyes.* She ends the message with three eye roll emojis.

Unfortunately, there isn't time for her suggestion because I'm pretty sure the woman I'm waiting on just walked through the door. Only she doesn't have red hair and everyone on the internet lies.

Her eyes do a quick sweep of the place and when they land on me, something hits me, something that feels a lot like a round kick straight to the gut. It feels like a throat punch in the wrong part of my body.

Immediately, I know it's her—my blind date—even though Nadia's description was off. She has caramel-colored hair, and she's tall and leggy, even without heels. She's also drop-dead gorgeous and definitely way out of my league.

When she offers a shy wave from across the room, my stomach sinks. Maybe I was hoping for a little disappointment, I don't know. Something akin to the others. This one, she's different. She's perfect, even without opening her mouth. Somehow I know this is true. She reminds me of Nadia's version of Beacon, where everyone is a ten, and not a two, like the version I've come to know.

She makes her way over and as she gets closer, there's something about her, something familiar. I note her white blouse and knee-length skirt, but I can't immediately place her.

She turns heads, that's for sure. She's refreshingly feminine. Slightly vulnerable and harmless—about as far from a cold-blooded killer as you can get. Looks can be deceiving, sure, but this time I can't be wrong. When she reaches the high-top table, she cocks her head and smiles. "Mark?"

Damn. It hits me then. I know her. Well, I don't *know* her, know her. It's complicated. Which is exactly how I make it. "Ali Brown?"

She looks surprised for a second, but not really. "Mark Lane?" The way she says my fake name seals the deal. She could be someone really special in my life. If circumstances were different. She's even better-looking in person than she is onscreen.

She extends her hand and I take it. "I thought your profile said Marie."

Color sweeps across her face. "Marie is my middle name."

"My ex-wife is a big fan," I say, vomiting foul words all over her. "I mean, she's a *huge* fan. She has all of your books. Some of them are signed. And the podcasts. She loves those, too."

She offers a tight smile, and I realize how much a person can fuck up in a mere two seconds. In my defense, I'm exhausted, I hate dating, and after three drinks, it's possible I could be slightly tipsy. "I'm sorry," I say. "I've made things awkward."

"It's fine."

"It's not fine. You're what? A sex therapist? So, it's not fine. If I tell you my ex-wife was a big fan—well—I'm sure the first thing you're thinking is what issues does he have."

She looks around for either a server or an exit, I can't be sure. "I wasn't thinking that."

She's not a great liar, that's for sure. Perspiration beads at my collar. I feel like a menopausal woman on a bad day, and I'm certain there are large pitstains on my shirt. Nadia was right. Wearing white was a terrible idea. "It's just, well, she's a lesbian, my ex. Something she left out for—oh, I don't know, ten years, give or take."

"I'm sorry."

"I'm not."

"Listen—actually, I *am* sorry. I've got to run."

"Of course," I say, racking my brain for something, *anything* I can come up with to get her to stay. I don't even know why. She's not alone in her need to bug out. I can't wait to escape either. Fight or flight has kicked in. I only know that I want—no—*have to* redeem myself. "I'm really sorry. I don't know what's gotten into me. It's just—I wasn't expecting you."

There's a slight furrow of her brow and a narrowing of her eyes, which I'm glad to see are actually green. I can tell she's pissed. It could be the lack of service. I could use another drink. "What were you expecting?"

"Well, you know how dating apps are."

"Do I?"

"I mean, usually it's just more of the same."

"Yes."

I make eye contact with the server who's giving me the full-on death stare and avoiding me because she realizes I am speed dating, rotating through women like glasses of gin, even though I told her more than once I'm looking for professional connections.

Ali glances at the door like she's desperate to leave. Suddenly logic prevails, and I realize why she lied about her name. "You must get recognized a lot."

"Sometimes."

The server appears and gives her the once-over. Ali glances at me and then back at the woman. "I can't stay," she says almost apologetically, but not quite.

"Just one drink?"

The server glares at me.

"You're not my type," Ali says firmly.

"How can you know?" The server rolls her eyes. "I mean, you just got here. And besides all the random fumbling with my words, we haven't even gotten a chance to talk. Give it a little time."

"I don't believe in wasting time. It's not personal."

"Really?" I motion between the two of us. "Because it feels kinda personal."

"It's a hunch," she says. "And my hunches are usually right." She stands and adjusts her skirt. "Thank you for your time, Mark." She smiles, and then she turns on her heel and walks out.

I shake my head at the server. "Networking sucks."

"Do you know who that was?" I ask Nadia as I fling the car door open and drop into the passenger seat. She looks over at me, one brow arched.

"A real killer, huh?"

"No, that was Ali Brown."

"Ali who?"

"Ali Brown. You know, the sex guru." I nod at the phone in her hand. "Look her up."

I watch her face as she studies the search results.

"She lied about her name," says Nadia. "And she schools men on eating box." She bites her bottom lip as she meets my eye. "Interesting."

"Eating box?"

"You know…jewel munching."

"What?"

She rolls her eyes. "Never mind."

"Wait. Oh, you mean—ah, I get it." Suddenly it makes so much sense why Bethany is such a fan. "Anyway—interesting and fucking gorgeous. But not our killer."

"How do you know?"

"She's too high profile."

"Well, I didn't know who she was. If she were high profile, I'd know her."

"Spoken like a true millennial."

She starts the ignition and glances over at me. She has a glint in her eyes that gives me second thoughts about letting her drive my car. Unfortunately, I have no choice. I'm not exactly sober.

"So, what now?"

"I don't know," I sigh. "We keep searching."

"You're terrible at dating, boss."

"Ali Brown. Do you think she's a lesbian?"

Nadia lifts her phone from her lap and types something in. After a bit of squinting at the screen, she looks over at me. "No, why?"

"I need to figure out how to get a second date."

"She's out of your league."

"I know."

CHAPTER TWELVE

Ali

Austin

Ali presses the button to record the session. The two people seated in front of her don't care. In fact, they hardly notice. That's how desperate they are to get laid.

Ali knows they aren't thinking about being recorded or what the repercussions may be. They've signed waivers and have zero qualms about having the intimate details of their lives available in audio for any and all to hear should that audio fall into the wrong hands. Stranger things have happened.

But Ali knows what most people don't. It's not sex they're looking for. It's acceptance. And in most cases, love, although many would settle for the former.

The couple that occupies her office, Jeff and Lisa, are having issues because Lisa came home early one day from a tennis lesson to find her husband dressed up in her clothes. Now that his secret is out of the bag, Jeff wants to bring his fetish into the bedroom, something that Lisa eventually reluctantly agreed to, but a habit that she could not sustain. When she suggested her husband take his proclivities elsewhere, he did for a short stint, and came home and found his wife and children had transferred themselves permanently to the couple's vacation home.

Jeff cannot understand why Lisa refuses to partake in his fantasies but refuses to allow them to play out elsewhere, and Lisa cannot understand why Jeff would put their relationship at risk. Eight sessions and thousands of dollars later, the couple is still at a stalemate.

When Ali brings up the issue of divorce, both Jeff and Lisa immediately shoot her down. "I just want to be accepted for who I am," Jeff says.

"And I," Lisa interjects, "I just want you to be who you *said* you were. When we met *and* when we married."

Ali closes her eyes briefly. No one wants to change, nor are they capable of budging on their positions.

"A divorce will not come cheap, either emotionally or finan-cially," Jeff adds.

Lisa nods. "We have young children to consider."

"I don't understand," Jeff says, glancing around the sparsely decorated office. Ali isn't sure what he's looking at. There are no diplomas on the wall, no personal artifacts. Just a couple of fake plants, three chairs, and a small coffee table. "She was into women in college."

Lisa's head jerks sideways. "That was *one* time!" She throws up her hands. "And how many times do I have to tell you? I was drunk."

Her husband shrugs and smiles smugly. It does not go unno-ticed by Ali that this couple is scorekeeping. He folds his hands across his chest and glares at his wife. "So get drunk."

"I married a man, Jeff. I want to fuck a man."

"You are," he scoffs.

KILL ME TOMORROW: A PSYCHOLOGICAL THRILLER

"A man in a dress is not a man."

Jeff has heard this before, Ali is sure of it, but he looks hurt. She can tell that he's about to strike back or say something explicit, but he seems to consider his audience. He's made his point, so he relents. Ali knows that Jeff is a good businessman. He's been incredibly successful in his professional life. He knows when to retreat.

"Is it possible that you could overlook the dress, Lisa, and just see your husband?"

"Maybe if he didn't insist on full makeup."

"What would happen if you let go of expectations and saw Jeff for who he is, the man that you married? Can you recall the first time the two of you met?"

Lisa usually had a fast answer for everything, but not this time. She didn't say a word. She went deep inside herself.

Ali waited.

Waves of emotion flowed across Lisa's face. Her frustration, her anger, and, beneath that, a deep sadness were palpable in the room. "But he isn't the man I married. He changed."

Ali offers a sympathetic smile. "We all change."

Lisa sat perfectly still in her chair. Ali could tell that she was testing what she said against her own logic. A verdict was imminent. "Not—" she motions toward her husband. "Not like this."

"You're angry. That's understandable." Lisa can't argue with Ali's assessment. She opens her mouth only to close it again, giving Ali the chance to speak. "Do you want to stay married?"

"That depends."

"On what?"

"On whether or not I'm supposed to live with a cross-dresser for the rest of my life."

Ali turns her gaze to Jeff. "What do you have to say about that, Jeff?"

Jeff isn't thinking about his answer. Ali knows this and Jeff knows it. He already knows deep in his core. Ali read the answers

71

on the homework assignments she assigned the couple. His responses are very different than his wife's.

He wrote two homework assignments ago that during their sessions he isn't thinking about meeting in the middle. He's thinking that he wishes he could go back in time and find someone like Ali. He is thinking that her hair looks nice today and that new dress she's wearing, it suits her. He's thinking about what it would be like to slip her out of it and whether she likes it fast and rough, or if he should take his time. His money is on it being the former. If he had just waited, he could have met someone more like her, and then he wouldn't be in this position. She may be soft on the outside, but he can see Ali for what she really is. For *who* she really is. She has a dark side, like him, a side that rebels against the norm, perhaps simply for the sake of doing so.

Ali didn't take the homework assignment personally. Not even when on his last assignment he got explicit. He wrote that a woman like Ali would let him pull her hair, she wouldn't lose her mind over a mark or two left behind. She wouldn't care whether he was wearing a dress or a three-piece suit. She wouldn't bat an eye at what he's into. His fetishes could probably change by the week and she still wouldn't care. They'd have a good laugh, she'd accept what is, they'd have a bit of fun and move on. Ali would give him what he wants, and he would take care of her. He could be happy with a woman like that.

It isn't true, of course. Ali is aware he just wants to get out of therapy. Jeff wants out of his marriage. He feels trapped in both, and he'll do anything to sabotage either.

Ali clears her throat. "Jeff?"

"I can't be someone I'm not."

"Well, that's a lie," Lisa says. "You're trying to be a woman and you're clearly not one."

Ali crosses and uncrosses her legs. She notices Jeff's stare. "You can understand, Jeff, that Lisa feels deceived."

He exhales long and slow and folds and unfolds his hands. Jeff told Ali that he thinks she does this on purpose, that she tries to get him to open up by using her sex appeal. He said it's one reason he doesn't mind paying her hourly rate. Also, he told her, it works. "Yeah, I understand that."

"And Lisa, you can understand how Jeff could feel unaccepted."

"No, not really. If he hadn't lied about who he really was—"

"But whatever the reason," Ali says. "He did lie. And so here we are. And now we have to figure out how to move forward."

Lisa stared at the floor. Jeff stared at Ali. In a few moments, Ali would know if she could proceed or not in bringing things to a close. She could feel Lisa's resistance, but she could also see that her face had softened, and that she looked visibly younger. Finally, the woman brightened and sat up a little straighter. "I'm not sure I can."

Ali glanced at Jeff and then met Lisa's eye. Jeff is not going to change. Lisa has to move toward acceptance. One way or the other, whether Lisa stays or she goes. Ali sighs. "You don't have a choice."

CHAPTER THIRTEEN

Ali

Austin

Ali sat at her desk, staring at her planner. Ali's favorite type of session is one in which her clients come to a resolution. Even if it doesn't feel that way on the surface, every session brings things closer to a head, to an ending, but more importantly to a new beginning.

She checks her schedule once again just in case her assistant has booked the two slots Ali keeps open on her calendar for emergencies. Thankfully, nothing has popped up, so four clients, two conference calls, and a podcast appearance are all that stands between Ali and her evening.

She has five minutes between appointments, just enough time to use the restroom and check her phone. She taps on one app and then another, making sure to hit all four. Beacon is her favorite. She always checks that one first, although sometimes the others surprise her and turn up something unexpected. There are hundreds of unread messages between the apps. Ten new ones in her Beacon inbox alone, just in the last hour. She knows she'll never catch up, so she looks for something that catches her eye instead. Something promising.

She thinks of Andrew from the flight and wonders what that would be like. Unfortunately, wrong city. At least for the moment, Andrew is geographically undesirable.

Ali has offices in three locations. Seattle, Boston, and Austin. This week she's in Texas, but she splits her time between the three cities. She also flies to meet clients where they are, often holding sessions in hotels, or rented spaces, but never in her client's homes. It's too personal and in her opinion, not conducive to therapy. To have any sort of real or meaningful breakthrough, you have to get a person out of their immediate situation and radically change their state.

The Beacon app pings, pulling her attention away from imagining Andrew and those curious eyes of his. When Ali taps the notification, she pauses. She recognizes the profile pic. It's the man from last night. Her first date of the evening. The one who recognized her. Ali liked him. Which was unfortunate because there was only one problem. He was too genuine. The kind who would only get hurt in the end.

She had better luck with her second date, although she had a third lined up if things took a turn for the worse. It turned out to be unnecessary. She went home with date number two. Lucas. Mid-twenties, trust fund baby with a tortured soul. She has a penchant for the type. She thought, at least initially, that this one might have the potential to be a regular, but as usual, she was disappointed in the end.

Hardly anyone turns out to be a regular. They either don't text back or they off themselves, something she supposes goes along with the tortured soul thing. It's fine about Lucas, whichever way it goes. The sex had been mediocre at best. An appetizer when what you really want is the main course. The fact that he cried almost made up for it, except that he came so fast, she nearly ended up in tears too.

Ali is not a crier.

She is thinking about Lucas, wondering what he might be like with a little coaching, if he'll ever realize what it means to be a good lover, or if he'll simply play shell games with one-night stands, when her assistant buzzes her to let her know her next clients have arrived.

There are techniques she could teach Lucas, but she knows it's pointless. You can't help everyone.

She starts to click her phone off, when the app pings again, notifying her of another message from Mark. She hesitates for a second before deleting it. Ali doesn't have time for genuine. She sees enough of that in her work. It pays well, because rarely do relationships turn out that way.

CHAPTER FOURTEEN

His apartment is dark and damp. Cluttered and full of filth. No place for a woman, that's for sure. What she saw in him is anyone's guess. What *any* woman sees, well, it's too much to try to comprehend. He isn't home when I arrive, but then, he rarely is. This is where he fucks and he sleeps, and as it turns out, it's where he'll die.

If he's surprised to come home and find me waiting, he doesn't show it. I think he must be high. It's the McDonald's bag in his hand at three in the morning that gives him away. He thinks it's a joke when I aim my gun at his head and order him to sit with his back against the wall. He doesn't beg. Instead, he has this curious look on his face. I can tell he thinks his buddies are playing a joke on him, that this is a prank. He's thinking about what a good story this will make.

Once he realizes he's mistaken, his demeanor doesn't shift all that much. He's certain I've come here to rob him, and a man like him values nothing. It reminds me of a poem written by Ryokan, a Zen master. He lived the simplest kind of life in a little hut at the foot of a mountain. One evening a thief visited the hut only to discover there was nothing in it to steal.

Ryokan returned and caught him. "You may have come a long way to visit me," he told the prowler, "and you should not return empty-handed. Please take my clothes as a gift."

Afterward, Ryokan sat naked, watching the moon. "Poor fellow," he mused. "I wish I could give him this beautiful moon."

Only this kid, he wouldn't give anyone the moon. He only thinks of himself, so I tell him to put the handgun in his mouth. It's not registered. Or maybe it is, who knows? That'll be a headache for someone else to figure out. I picked it up for fifty bucks off the street from a guy who looked like he hadn't slept for days.

It takes a bit of coaching to get him to put it in his mouth, and I have to prove that the clip is empty. Of course the chamber isn't, but he's a hipster. He doesn't know that. I'd be surprised if he's ever touched a gun in his life.

He starts to freak out a little. Just a tinge of panic. Nothing I haven't seen before. Nothing I can't handle. I tell him he has to trust me. *Why would I hand him a loaded gun? How stupid would that be?*

This seems to be logic he understands, but only because it's rooted in emotion. He takes the gun out of his mouth and tells me he doesn't have any money on him, but that he can get some, whatever I need. The way he says it makes me smile. It's naive, almost like he doesn't mind handing over what's his. Like the Zen master, he considers it charity, but he's different. His possessions aren't his. He's done nothing, added nothing to society. Another thing he's never done in his young life—put in a hard day's work, which is probably why he thinks he can fuck with people's emotions, why he's a terrible lover, why he's a disgrace. In a world full of Mickey D's, McSex, McRelationships, where everything is fast, easy, and cheap, not to mention ready to trash when it's slightly inconvenient, he thinks he's different. He thinks his art will get him somewhere in life, but nothing worth having was ever made in a few minutes in the drive-thru lane.

To drive my point home, I ask him to put on one of his EPs. He thinks I am genuinely interested, but I think it will be nice to have him die with a familiar soundtrack in the background. Not to mention it'll look good on the police report.

I ask him to pour us a drink. He stands and reluctantly goes around to the kitchen. I watch as he lays the pistol on the counter and mixes two cocktails. He doesn't touch his. I down mine and shove the glass in my jacket pocket. A souvenir, I say to him. With a nod, I tell him it'll be a great story when he's famous. *Maybe he could autograph it?*

He smiles at that. Once again, I tell him to put the revolver in his mouth. The first time you get a person to do something they don't want to do, it can be hard. The second time is always easier; it's a little like boiling a frog. I tell him I'd like a picture. It could make a great album cover. I've always had an eye for art.

He laughs and I can see his fragile ego is stroked. My proof is, he picks up the gun and he does what I ask. Although, when I tell him to pull the trigger, he doesn't so easily acquiesce. The secondary weapon in my left pocket might help, but I'd rather not go there. This has to be his idea. It feels better that way.

He stalls by taking the gun from his mouth to ask if I'd like another drink. I wouldn't, but he pours two anyway, one for him and one for me. I don't mind. I've got time.

We listen to his shit music as he finishes his drink. "I've got to get going," I say. "How about that photo?"

"I know I'm buzzing," he laughs. "But this is too much." He cocks his head and narrows his eyes. "Chris put you up to this?"

"Who's Chris?"

He points a finger at me. "Good one."

After a moment of silence, he gives in and positions the gun in his mouth. "How's this?" he asks as I adjust my phone into position. His mouth opens wider and he looks at me with a sort of wry grin.

"Finger on the trigger," I tell him, angling the camera. "Make it look real."

He does as I ask, and then jokingly, he squeezes the trigger. Only it isn't a joke, and the chambered bullet works its magic. My God, if it isn't a mess.

CHAPTER FIFTEEN

Ethan

I'm in the drop-off line at school with the kids when the police department number shows up on caller ID. It's Max, or at least I hope it is. Max is my best friend. We worked together as rookies at the police department a long time ago, ages ago, before I joined the FBI. While my life has taken many turns, Max is still there, now as a lead detective. Without thinking, I place the call on speaker, forgetting that the conversation will play throughout the car. "Ethan," Max says, breathless. "We got another one."

I don't even get in a hello.

"Last night. Some kid blew his brains out."

Goddamn it. I glance in the rearview mirror. Max's revelation just so happened to coincide perfectly with the timing of the safety patrol opening my car door. Not only did my children hear about a dead kid, half of the school courtyard has too.

"A kid?" I sigh, ducking to peer out the passenger window at Kelsey. "I told you—my range is twenty-five to sixty-five." I fish

Kelsey's lunch box from the backseat and hand it to her out the window.

"Well, not a *kid* kid. He's—I don't know—twenty-two, twenty-three."

I consider it for a second. "Nah, I don't think so. The others were older."

"Look," he tells me with a huff. "I don't know why you're busting my balls. You're the one who said if anything that so much as smelled like a suicide popped up, you wanted to know about it."

Kelsey stands at the door. She flashes me a quick smile as she flings her backpack over her shoulder. I watch as she hurries off to find her classmates. "Was there a note?"

"Hang on a minute." I hear the phone fall away from his ear and then him typing on, knowing Max, what is an undoubtedly outdated computer. "No, I don't think so. The report's not final yet, though."

"Okay." I search the sea of children for a familiar head of hair, a set of shoulders I know like the back of my hand. Finally, my eyes land on Nick, and I wave. He pretends not to notice. "Send it over, I'll take a look."

"Lane, look—I know I owe you—but...um...this one I'll need to get to you a different way. Sorry, but I can't risk it. You'll have to meet me in person."

"Why?"

"He's a senator's son."

I'M NEARLY TO THE OFFICE WHEN THE SCHOOL'S NUMBER APPEARS on my screen. I answer, expecting to hear Nick on the other end of the line telling me he forgot his lunch on the kitchen counter, so I'm surprised by the raspy smoker's voice I know belongs to the school counselor. She introduces herself as though we haven't spoken half a dozen times and then she says, "I have Kelsey here in my office. She's very upset. And I was hoping you might have time to come in and speak with me. Perhaps we could all meet together?"

"Now? I just dropped her off."

"If you wouldn't mind coming back to the school, that would be great."

"I'm sorry," I tell her. "I've just pulled into work."

"Perhaps I should call your wife?"

"Ex-wife," I tell her. "And no. I'm sorry. I don't have the time to turn around and come back and no, you should most definitely not call Bethany. Anyway, she's out of town."

"Kelsey is upset about her behavior at morning assembly," the counselor tells me amid several coughing fits. "In fact, she's more than upset. She's crying and inconsolable."

"What happened at morning assembly?" Kelsey doesn't have behavior issues.

"I'm not entirely sure. All I know is, her teacher sent her to my office because she's embarrassed about weeping in the middle of the moment of silence, and she wants to come home."

"May I speak with her?"

I hear sniffles as Kelsey comes on the line. "Kelsey? What's going on?"

"I'm scared."

My heart sinks. I thought we were past this. "What happened?"

"You're going to die. And then who will pick me and Nick up from school?"

"I'm not going to die."

"Yes you are. The bad guy is going to kill you. Or the bad girl. Like you said."

"I didn't say that, Kelsey. No one is going to kill me." I hate to hear my child cry. But it's funny, a five-year-old's logic. She's only thinking about today, not the entirety of her life and what my absence might mean. "Can you give the phone back to Mrs. Rawlings?"

"So, you're on your way then?"

"My ex-wife is on a business trip. I'm sure Kelsey is just missing her mother."

"Change can be difficult for children."

"Yes, and I have to admit, I didn't exactly enforce a proper bedtime last night."

"She's probably just tired."

"What do you think it might take to get her back to class?" I ask with a sigh. "I have a meeting at the police station." This isn't entirely true, but I do need to meet Max and get the information he is providing on the down low.

I hear a shift in the counselor's breathing. I cross my fingers, hoping that I've done enough to make it sound important and official, even though it's anything but. I only know that I cannot miss work. I am barely keeping the lights on as it is, and what goes on in my office is no place for a little girl. "Hello?" I say. I don't even hear the raspy cough, just a dead silence.

"Hold, please."

"I'm sorry," the woman tells me firmly when she comes back on the line. "I am aware of your profession and the importance of your work. But, your daughter is inconsolable, Mr. Lane, and this is what it means to be a parent."

Her brutal honesty shocks me at first, not to mention the fact that she used my exact words against me, practically verbatim. I feel the familiar build of acid creeping up my throat and I get angry. "I'm curious, Miss. What's it mean to be a counselor these days? Where *do* all of those taxpayer dollars go?"

"Great. We'll see you soon then," she quips into the phone. If I didn't know better, I swore I heard a smile in her voice.

So this is how I end up with a child camped under my desk, doing my best to field her incessant questions between conference calls.

Besides the Roberts case, which, if I play it right, will be my bread and butter, I am working several contracts with insurance companies that have gone nowhere, mostly from lack of attention. It takes a lot of effort to tail people and to report their comings and goings. It's not exactly a cakewalk cataloguing and photographing the details of people's personal lives. The contracts include weekly conference calls with the insurance agencies to provide status updates, and today my schedule is jam-packed. We go case by case; me relaying the evidence I've collected, the attorneys offering additional personal information, addresses, anything that might be beneficial. The goal is for me to gather evidence, to take photos or video in order to prove fraudulent claims. That, or to obtain anything, any information that might cause a party to settle. It's low-grade work, work that any investigator can do, but it puts food on the table, and at this point, even though I don't enjoy it, I can't afford to turn it down.

Kelsey's face lights up when I ask if she's up for a stakeout, which in actuality means trailing folks that have insurance claims against companies who will do whatever it takes not to pay claims. Typically, my work is not a family affair, but since Bethany thought that accompanying her girlfriend on a business trip would be a grand idea, what else am I supposed to do?

"Maybe we'll stop by and see Uncle Max."

Her expression shifts.

I grab her backpack and my camera bag. "Or we don't have to."

"Remember what Mommy said?"

I tread carefully because there's no telling. "What did Mommy say?"

"She said you weren't supposed to do work around us. She said that's why we can't see you very much anymore because you're always working."

"I'm not always working, love. But I have a very important case that I need to solve. It would help a lot of people. Helping people is good, isn't it?"

"Is it because of what Uncle Max said?"

I narrow my gaze. "What Uncle Max said?"

"He said there was a dead kid."

It hits me then why she was so upset this morning. I shouldn't have picked up that call. I should have been more careful. Sometimes I think that what Bethany says is true. I am not cut out to be a father. I bend at the knee, meeting her at eye level. "No honey, it wasn't a child. Uncle Max just used the wrong word."

Her brow furrows.

"Look—Uncle Max is old. To him, anyone under forty is a kid. It's slang. Have you learned about slang words yet at school?"

"I don't believe you," she tells me, folding her arms across her chest. "Mommy is right. You always lie."

CHAPTER SIXTEEN

Ethan

I t's so cold and so dark. It's the bitter chill, the deep ache in my bones, that wakes me. I assume the power must have gone out or the heater is on the fritz.

I hear sounds coming from outside, like a door or a window has been left open, but I know that it's something far worse. I make a move to climb out of bed. The next thing I know, I feel nothing. Something, or rather someone, hits me over the head. The crack is a sound I will not soon forget. I see a face flash in front of mine and then everything goes dark. I have no idea for how long, only that it seems like forever. I go in and out of consciousness, and the sensation feels strongly like being forced under water, only to be brought back up again.

The next time my eyes flutter open, it is to the sound of a child's cries. Nick. He cries off and on and then he mumbles something. I can't make out what, only that he's repeating the same sentence over and over. I don't know if it's the blood that has filled my ears, or if my hearing has been permanently impacted by the blow to my head, I just know that my son's words sound far off and that they are being spoken too fast for me to make them out.

I fight not to be pulled under by the darkness once again. It's a battle to stay on the edge, half in this world, half of me wanting to give in. I can hear Bethany's voice and that brings me back and holds me in place. She is pleading, but more than that, her voice is angry. She is arguing with someone. Then she is screaming my name.

I try to move. I try to shift, to stand, to push myself up and out of bed. I have to get to her. I don't know what is going on, only that whatever it is, that whoever has forced their way into our home and tied me up and bludgeoned me, is not here to make friends. My head swims. It feels dull and heavy. My feet and wrists are bound. I should know what to do. I've been trained for this, but none of the information is easily accessible. Pain has made my recall nonexistent.

Eventually, I drift back into nothingness. I don't want to, I fight it, but it's no use. The darkness takes me anyway.

I awake to hushed voices speaking rapidly down the hall. I no longer hear Nicky's cries, but one voice belongs to Bethany. Our bedroom door is open and in the next room, I hear Bethany giving instructions. Numbers. Banking information. Based on the bits of the conversation, I make out that she is at the computer. She always has issues with that computer. Suddenly, I feel dizzy. They are going to kill her. I turn my head to the left and puke all over the sheets my wife proudly brought home just last week. I'm so tired. If it weren't so cold and if my wrists and feet weren't bound and if my wife weren't about to die, I might just go back to sleep. But I don't go back to sleep. I know that I have to find a way out of this room, out of this bed, out of these restraints. I know enough to know this isn't a simple robbery. I saw the perp's face before he knocked me out. It's one I've seen before, one that is etched in my memory. It's the same face I put behind bars three years ago. He did not come here simply for money. Men like him never do.

According to the clock on the wall, it takes me eight minutes to free myself from the restraints and the bedroom. The first thing I do once I've freed my hands is reach for the drawer in the nightstand. I fish for the gun only to find it missing, which isn't surprising. It's efficient, but a terrible hiding spot. I grab the one in my T-shirt drawer instead.

Instinct kicks in. I take inventory as to what I'm up against. I flip the power switch. Nothing happens. The power has been cut, and the alarm did not sound. The intruders are not amateurs. Keeping me alive has been their first mistake. Hopefully they've made others.

Slowly, I move toward the door, tiptoeing quietly, carefully. Unfortunately, in my haste I am not careful enough. I bump the lamp at the end of the dresser and it crashes to the floor. The one Bethany's mother gave us as a housewarming gift, the one my wife insisted on keeping just in case her mother ever asked about it. I hated that lamp from the first time I saw it. Now it lies broken on the floor. Now it has given me away.

I round the corner quick, gun drawn, counting the men within eyesight. There are two. One is standing over Bethany, who is seated at the small desk built into the wall between the kitchen and the dining room. He's staring back at me, wide-eyed. I am guessing he is not the one tasked with making sure I stayed in bed. He positions the pistol at her temple, a clear warning.

The other man has his weapon trained on my children. Nick and the girls are on the loveseat, huddled together, their eyes glassy, their faces mostly blank. It's apparent they are in shock.

Bethany has her back to me. She argues with the man standing over her, insisting, *swearing* that the password she is typing in is correct. She promises she isn't lying.

She isn't.

I know my wife and I know how bad she is with numbers. She can't remember a password to save her life. Obviously. Our household finances have always been my job. Bethany has never cared to be involved.

I shift my stance, training my gun on the man seated opposite my children, calculating how fast I will need to be to kill both men. If it's just the two of them, I might have a shot.

My hand isn't as steady as I'd like it to be, but it helps that I'm running on nerves and adrenaline. My training has kicked in. Lining up my sight, I take aim. Abby sees me and she shouts my name, and all hell breaks loose. I fire, hitting the man closest to my children in the shoulder. But I don't stop there. I empty my clip into the both of them. Everything happens fast, but it feels like slow motion.

Bethany falls to the floor and then claws her way under the desk. I rush toward our children. The intruders have toppled everything over, and I am not that steady on my feet. It's a strange thought, but I realize I will ever only know bits and pieces of whatever has happened in this room.

Nick runs toward his mother. The girls don't move. Abby is slumped over onto Kelsey, her face buried in her sister's chest. At first I think she is crying, or hiding, or both. When I reach down to lift her up, I feel the warmth, and I know. She's been shot. When I look down, I see Kelsey is covered in blood. Abby rolls in my arms, her head flopping backward over my arm. Her eyes are fixed open. They stare at the ceiling. I shake her before I drop to the floor. I feel for a pulse, although I know I won't find one. I know my daughter is dead. But that still doesn't stop me from trying to save her, from ripping her once pink pajamas open and performing CPR. I hear Bethany's screams and I feel Kelsey tugging at the sleeve of my shirt. "Daddy," she whispers. "Abby is dead. Mommy is bleeding."

"Daddy!"

I feel a hand on my chest. It shakes me. "Dad, wake up."

I open my eyes to find my children standing over me. Nick looks alarmed, and Kelsey has tears streaming down her face. "Daddy, you're doing it again."

I REAR UP, UNTIL I'M SITTING FULLY UPRIGHT. I CLUTCH MY CHEST and try to catch my breath, and when it doesn't work, I ease back against the headboard like a cornered animal. I am covered in sweat. I am certain a heart attack is imminent. This is more than reflux. I am going to die. And my children are going to witness it.

"It's just a bad dream," Nick says, forcing the glass of water that was on my nightstand in my face. "Breathe."

My hands are shaking too much to take the glass, so I wave him off, wiping the sweat from my brow. Nick counts backwards from ten. "Slow deep breaths, like the doctor said."

He's talking about the therapist, not an actual medical doctor, and I don't know when he grew up, but I do as he requests, inhaling deeply and exhaling slowly.

When the shortness of breath passes, I lift the covers, and Kelsey climbs into bed with me. I expect Nick to follow suit. But he doesn't. He stares at me, a little frightened, but also with a disappointed look on his face. "You're okay now?"

"I'm fine," I say, inching over. I pat the spot next to me. "Are you sure you don't want to come in?"

"You talk in your sleep," he tells me, as he shakes his head. "I'm going back to bed."

"Should I come tuck you in?"

He gives me a look. A look that reminds me of his mother. "Just help Kelsey get back to sleep. Mom will be pissed if she falls asleep in class again."

"You shouldn't use that language," I say. It's important to remind him I'm still his father, even if he has outgrown my bed, even if he has assumed the caretaker role in this moment. He may think he is too old and too tough to need me, that perhaps I need him more, but he is wrong. "Goodnight," I add. "Thank you for the water."

"Tell me a story," Kelsey says, watching Nick retreat from the room. "But Dad?"

"Yeah?"

"I think we should keep the light on. You don't have nightmares when the lights are on."

"Okay, we'll leave them on."

I lift the iPad from the nightstand and check the cameras. Nick is in bed, but he isn't laying down. He's seated at the foot, staring at the floor. I should probably go to him, but something tells me to give him a moment. Nick has always been the kind of kid who needs to process things before he can talk about them. I've learned not to push him. I wish I could say the same for his mother.

"Remember what Dr. Nancy says?"

"Yes," I say. It could be anything.

"She says it's okay to be afraid of the dark."

"That's right." I pat her head. "How about that story?"

"Tell me about me and Abby," she says, and my breath hitches in my throat. "About when we were born."

"All right. Well, let's see. It was a beautiful day. The doctor said that if you weren't born by the second week in April that they were going to induce."

"In—what?"

"They were going to force you out. You were late for twins. Your mother was running out of room in her belly for the both of you."

She smiles, even though she's heard this story dozens of times. It's the same story I always tell her, about the day she and her sister were born. It's the only one I can allow my heart to touch. I tell her how the nurse placed two tiny pink bundles in my arms. I tell her how it felt like holding two footballs; they were so tiny and so light.

Her favorite part of the story is when I tell her how she wrapped her itty-bitty wrinkled hand around my index finger and held on. She likes it when I tell her how she was the one who was wide awake from the start, how she was always wide awake, refusing to miss a second of anything, while her sister was the perfect sleeper.

Someday I will tell her the rest, but now she snuggles into the crook of my arm, not so unlike the day she was born, and closes her eyes. I close mine too. I don't sleep, I can't sleep. In a second, I'll check in on Nicky. For now, I allow my mind to drift back to the past, but only to safe territory.

I think about how Bethany tried and tried to get pregnant after Nick, about the days of injections, the weeks of doctor appointments and blood draws. Month after month, when the tests turned out negative, she sunk further and further into a funk she couldn't seem to climb out of.

I hadn't been particularly concerned. Getting pregnant with Nick was so easy it was practically an accident, and I was convinced that it would happen again just the same, when the time was right. But Bethany, being the type A personality that she is, insisted on seeing a fertility specialist.

She was adamant that we go through with treatment, even though we hadn't been trying that long. It didn't matter that the hormones made her crazy or drove her deeper and deeper into a depression. A depression so deep that I pleaded with her to stop the injections, or at the very least hit the pause button. We had time. We had one healthy baby; I didn't understand why she needed to put herself through all of that for another.

Her insistence almost wrecked our marriage. I thought of leaving, even though I wouldn't have. There was Nicky, and I loved my wife. I'd sit at my desk at work, afraid to go home, afraid of what I might find. I daydreamed about inventing a time machine. Instead, I took a months-long assignment out of town. Bethany was furious that I would go, seeing that we were trying to conceive and my absence could set us back.

When I went anyway, she suggested that I not come back, that it be a trial separation. I figured it was the hormones talking, and the stress, not that I disagreed entirely.

Thankfully, it felt like divine intervention when two weeks into the trip, Bethany called to say that her test that morning showed two faint lines. Several weeks later it was confirmed, we were having twins.

About a month or so after we found out I arrived home, and we threw a party in our backyard, surprising our family and closest friends with the news. Bethany's pregnancy with the girls was a lovely time, almost like a second honeymoon for us. I've never been more proud of my wife than when I was watching her carry my daughters. I fell in love with her all over again when she delivered two perfect, healthy baby girls. The moment they were placed in my arms was the greatest moment of my life. I hadn't expected it to be better than it had been with Nick, but it was. Our family was now complete. We had the rest of our lives ahead of us.

CHAPTER SEVENTEEN

Ethan

Ali stands at the gas pump wearing a perfect dress and a pensive expression. The neon from the station sign overhead partially shades one side of her face, giving her a devilish look. I watch as she positions the nozzle in her tank and presses the lever, which refuses to stick. It takes three tries before she realizes that she's forgotten to select the grade of fuel she wants.

She jabs at the button, shakes her head, and turns and leans back against the car, folding her arms across her chest. After several seconds, she sighs, opens the driver's side door and reaches into the car and grabs her cell phone. She starts scrolling, even though there are signs posted all over warning of the dire consequences of doing such a thing. She's a rebel. It's probably better I know that now. I strain, trying to catch a glimpse of her screen, but I can't manage it, so I wait for her to stop scrolling and look up. Her body language makes it obvious what she is thinking. She's nervous. She should be. She should know better. She ought to be aware of her surroundings. It's dangerous for her to be on her phone, dangerous in more ways than one. Convenience stores at night are not exactly the safest places in the world for anyone, let alone for a woman who looks like Ali.

I shuffle my feet and shift my balance, hoping she'll notice. Her scrolling is endless, and my tank is full.

"Ali?"

My voice catches her off guard. She nearly drops the phone. But she recovers quickly, glancing over her shoulder, her brows raised.

"Sorry," I say. I lift my hands so that my palms face her. "I didn't mean to startle you."

"I wasn't startled." She looks toward the pump and back at me. "I just wasn't expecting to hear my name."

She clicks off her phone and sizes me up. She has the most stunning green eyes I've ever seen. Cat-like and curious. Trouble for sure. "Mark, right?"

"You remember?"

"How could I forget?"

"I don't know," I say. "Maybe because I sent three messages and they've all gone unread."

"I've been busy." Ali doesn't apologize the way most women would. But her eyes dart from side to side in a manner that suggests she's aware that she's in a dimly lit place with a man whose advances she has thwarted. Her response to me seems softer than it might be otherwise.

"I'm sure." My eyes flit toward my car. "Anyway, I didn't mean to bother you. I saw you standing there and thought I'd say hello."

"Your bio," she says, sucking on her bottom lip. "On the app. Did you write that?"

I shake my head. "My assistant did. She's always saying I need to get back out there. Clearly she's mistaken, after our disaster of a date."

"You mean the date where you couldn't stop talking about

KILL ME TOMORROW: A PSYCHOLOGICAL THRILLER

your ex-wife?" She waves one hand in the air, brushing me off. "No, it was great."

"No it wasn't. But I was hoping for another shot."

She looks down at her phone. She's having second thoughts. Later she would tell me that she hadn't remembered me having a voice this deep or a jawline this cut, but then the bar had been noisy and she was distracted. Ali looked back at me. I notice her features are symmetrical and the youthful glow she has to her cheeks. The dress she's wearing is yellow, three-quarter sleeved and lacy. I wonder where she's going or where else she's been in a dress like that. She smiles. "Okay."

"Okay?"

"You wanna go for a drink?"

I lift my chin. "Now?"

"Well, I have to wait for my gas to finish pumping, but yes, now."

"I thought you said I wasn't your type."

A smile creeps across her face. "What can I say?" She nods toward my vintage Porsche, a gift from Bethany's dad. A gift I am lucky to get to continue to "borrow" as part of the divorce settlement. "I really like that car."

CHAPTER EIGHTEEN

Ali

Austin

Ethan drives her to The Crispy Biscuit where he orders his favorite, green eggs and ham. Ali orders a gimlet. She smiles and fingers the rim of her glass. "Dr. Seuss was cancelled, you know."

"Cancelled?"

"Yeah, they stopped printing his books. And worse, they announced it on his birthday."

"That's terrible."

She shrugs, sinking deeper into the booth. "It depends on who you ask."

"A sign of the times, I suppose." He stuffs·a forkful of ham into his mouth. "I wonder how long it will remain on the menu. I hope they don't ban ham."

"Yeah." She leans forward and steals a piece of egg from his plate. "You better live it up. You come here often, Mark? Wait—" she squints. "I've forgotten your last name."

He stops midbite. "You left your car at a gas station and rode to a secondary location with a man whose last name you don't know. Voluntarily."

She shrugs and lifts her gimlet, signaling cheers. "Like I said, life is short."

"Shorter if you make a habit of getting into cars with strangers."

"You're only sort of a stranger. Technically, this is our second date."

"You call this a date?"

"I haven't decided yet."

The waitress refills his water, while giving Ali the side eye.

"A friend of yours?" Ali asked, brow raised, after the woman waddled off.

"That's Barbie."

"So her nametag said. And you're what? Your bio said—hold on, don't tell me—a dentist? No, an attorney. That's right." Ali shifts in the booth, sitting straight up. She leans in close. "What kind of law?"

He sticks close to the truth. "I represent insurance companies, mostly. Devils that they are."

"Ah." She studies him curiously. This diner is not where she expected him to take her. *He* is not what she expected.

"And you?"

Ali smiles, fingering the rim of her glass. She's heard all the usual first date questions. She's used to this. *Where do you see yourself in five years? Do you believe in love? Do you want children? How do you feel about marriage?*

KILL ME TOMORROW: A PSYCHOLOGICAL THRILLER

She'll answer honestly. Just not *too* honestly. Ali doesn't believe in love. But she won't tell him that. For Ali, love is nothing more than a projection people place on one another, a projection of themselves and how they feel at any given moment. As for marriage, she sees it as a set of expectations, nothing more than a contractual agreement held in place by good intentions and a court of law. The intention she understands. It's the expectations she dislikes. So many expectations, some personal, most societal, or familial, many of them unconscious. She finds it all very nauseating. And as for children, that's a hard no. But she won't say any of that. What's the point? Chances are she's never going to see this guy again after tonight. "You know what I do."

"But *I* haven't read your books."

"Pity."

"Do you enjoy it?"

Her eyes narrow. She wants to ask what he means. *Does she like sex and loose strings?* Yes. Very much. For Ali, those two things go hand in hand. They're about as honest as you can get. It's a shame sex has to come with a slew of expectations, expectations that are easily finagled and very hard to untangle. "I do very well in my professional life."

"That wasn't what I asked."

Ali smiles at his bluntness. You can learn a lot about people by simply observing them. Especially while they're on their best behavior, which let's face it, in the beginning of any relationship, everyone is. But this one, he's testing her. And she likes it. "You want to know if I find pleasure in my job?"

"Well, do you?"

"Sometimes."

"For example—"

"You aren't very good at dating. This feels like a job interview."

"Does it?"

"How about we get outta here?"

103

"You haven't even tried their pie. It's to die for."

Ali swallows hard. She's never wanted to take a man and drag him out of a place before. But she supposes there's a first time for everything. She doesn't care about pie or food. All she can think about is ripping off his white button-down and finding out what's underneath. "We can have dessert at your place."

"My place?"

"Is that a problem?"

It's her way of asking if he has a wife or a girlfriend. Even a situationship could mess her night up. She likes to know up front. Women can fake orgasms, but men can fake entire relationships.

"It's not a problem," he tells her. "My place is fine. But first—"

"First what?"

"First you have to answer the question."

She rolls her eyes and then signals Barbie for pie and the check. "Fine." She leans in and lowers her voice. "You want to know what *really* gives me pleasure?"

"Yes."

"I'm trying to show you and you want me to put it in words?"

"That's exactly what I want you to do. And not *what* gives you pleasure. You said that. I want to know what about your job you enjoy. Forgive me. I'm a fan of specifics."

"Clearly." Ali ponders his question while picking slivers of ham off his plate. "In my work, I don't study what people say. I study what they do."

"And that tells you what?"

"It tells me whether I can help them. It tells me if they even want help to begin with."

"And you help them how?" He leans forward resting his elbows on the table. "Considering they want it."

"Well, if you find what makes a person tick—what *truly* makes them tick, beyond surface level stuff—and you can provide that, then the rest is easy. But people don't always want to give up their wants and desires so easily."

"Tell me about it."

"Hell, half the time they don't even know what they are them-selves. And let me tell you something, Mark. Most people who are looking for love, or for marriage, or even a one-night stand, they're only doing it hoping it will make them feel better. So when I can cut through all of that—when we cut through the bullshit—and get to the core, that's when my work pleases me."

"And what is it that most people want?" Barbie places a slice of pie in front of him and hands him the check. He looks up at her and smiles and then slides a fork to Ali. "When you cut through the bullshit?"

"Besides pie?" Ali shifts back in her seat. "That's easy. What I just said. They want to feel better."

"And they expect *you* to make that happen?"

"That's what they pay me for, yes."

"And all you're doing is talking."

"I listen."

"Sounds easy enough."

"Not always. But most people aren't as different as they think they are."

"It doesn't stop there, though, does it?"

"What do you mean?" *I don't sleep with my clients, except for the one. And that was a mistake.*

"I mean, you have to keep trying to make them feel better. Keep coming up with things that surprise them, until the inevitable day comes, which is really a very sad day, really. The day they learn that no one else can truly make them happy. They have to do that for themselves. Of course, by that point they will believe it's *you*. They'll make sure you know it's you. That's the source of their unhappiness. It will be something that you've done, something that you changed, or started, and this is the beginning of the end. From there it's a downhill snowball."

Her eyes widen. "That's exactly how it is. How'd you know?"

"Call it a good guess."

"No, really." She pulls the pie a little closer to her side of the table and pinches off a piece of the crust.

He shrugs. "It sounds a lot like love."

CHAPTER NINETEEN

Ethan

After Abby died, I promised myself I would never take on a criminal case again, and I haven't. For a long time, insurance fraud became my area of expertise. Then Camille Roberts contacted me. The truth is, I was bored with insurance work and workers comp claims. And more than that, I couldn't afford to turn Camille down. Even if I'd wanted to. So I took the job. What I wanted, aside from not being a complete and total public failure, was one last great criminal case. Proof that I still had it in me.

I don't know if that's what this case will turn out to be. The only thing I do know is that Camille is difficult. She's the kind of woman who throws a wrench into all your plans and finds satisfaction in the undertaking. But she pays well. She's a woman on a mission, and I have to respect that. It was Camille who said that no stone can be left unturned, and that is exactly how I find myself in the car, driving toward my house with a woman I met on the internet, a woman that could be responsible for the murder of not just one man, but several.

I consider the odds that Ali Brown killed Donovan Roberts or any of the other men. It's probably not a very smart game plan to come right out and ask. She has several strikes against her. For one, she has offices in two of the four cities the victims lived in. Two, I did copy almost word for word the bios of the previous victims, hoping to catch the killer's interest. I try to come up with a third strike and can't. At least not yet. It doesn't help that all I can think about is the beautiful woman in my passenger seat, wearing the best dress I've ever seen, who is probably most likely going to have sex with me and, well, I can't force myself to care about anything else.

What I can do is call Nadia and relay my current situation, just in case I fail to turn up at work in the morning.

When we get to my house, I'm relieved Ali asks to use the bathroom. I call Nadia. Three rings in, I pray she picks up. She doesn't on the first try, so I frantically call again. She finally answers on my third call, out of breath and annoyed. "This better be good—"

"Ali Brown is in my bathroom," I whisper-scream into the phone.

"What?"

"The woman you set me up with from the app. She's here."

"At your house?"

"That's right."

"What the fuck, boss?" There's a brief pause and when I don't answer she adds, "Thinking with your dick is going to get you killed!"

All women say that, but this time Nadia has a point.

"I picked up the file from Max." She lets out a quick sigh. "Let's just say you should not be alone with this woman. If I were you, I wouldn't be alone with any woman from that app. Not so long as you're plagiarizing the bios of dead guys."

"Wait. Max gave you the file? On the senator's kid?"

"Lucas Bennett. Yeah, why?"

"Really?"

"You know I have a way of getting what I want." Anyone else's voice would be proud, but Nadia's is void of emotion.

"Wow." I'm scared to ask what she did to get Max to hand over the file. Max has gotten itchy lately, with good reason. We all know he can't keep compromising himself the way he has been.

"He—"

"No, it's okay. Stop there, I really don't want to know."

I hear the toilet flush and the faucet turn on. "Listen, I have to go. I just wanted you to know who I'm with in case—"

I don't finish my sentence because I spot Ali's handbag lying on the chair in my living room. I walk over to it, the phone pressed to my ear. I lean down and open the flap, knowing full well that she could come out of that restroom at any second. "Gotta go," I say into the phone. "Fingers crossed, I see you tomorrow. Don't forget the file."

"Don't do it," I hear Nadia say right before I end the call. I shove the phone in my back pocket and rifle through the contents of Ali's purse. Inside there's a wallet, a tube of lipstick, a tampon and—what the fuck? *A handgun.*

CHAPTER TWENTY

Ethan

My heart starts racing. My palms grow sweaty. Fight or flight kicks in. I have my Glock on me and years of aikido at my disposal and still my throat sticks. This woman is a possible murderer, and she's in my house. *Fuck, what am I going to do?*

I could just ask her to leave. I could tell her I'm not feeling well. But no. That would make too much sense, and at the moment I still want to get laid. I have a gun, she has a gun. I'm not a killer, she might not be a killer.

Just in case, I need a "Plan B." So I go into the kitchen, take the bottle of sleeping pills prescribed to me by a doctor I never see, pills that I never touch, and crush one into a million tiny pieces, until they're finer than a grain of sand. I fetch two wineglasses from the cabinet, glasses I never use, and open an old bottle of red. I fill the glasses, dropping the powder into one of them.

Remnants of the pills float at the top, so I stick my finger in the glass and stir like mad.

When I hear the creak of the bathroom door, I take the glasses in my hand and round the bar into the living room. *Right hand, I live. Left hand, I die.*

She appears from the hall and crosses into the living area and I get the chance to take her in, in a way that I hadn't at the diner. She looks out of place in this house, with its walls that need painting and flooring that could use an update. Ali fumbles with the silk tie on her dress, pulling it tighter, wrapping it around her, forming it into a bow. She's breathtaking. She could wear a paper sack and easily be the most beautiful woman in any room, and potentially, I remind myself, the most deadly.

I hand her the glass. She takes it from me only to set it on the bar. "I don't really mix liquor and wine," she smiles. "I'm a bit of a lightweight."

Somehow I doubt that. My gut told me she wouldn't touch it. I'm relieved. My paranoia shouldn't have let me chance it. Too big a risk drugging a woman these days. No one's going to believe you when you say you thought she might kill you in your own home. And yet, it happens every day.

"You have kids." It's not a question, the way she says it. More like a tight-lipped accusation.

"Three—two, now," I say, not knowing how to answer. I never know how to answer that question. Telling the truth is heavy, but omitting Abby feels like pretending she never existed, and that stabs at my heart, so usually I end up tripping over my words instead, making things worse.

Her brow lifts. She's waiting for me to say more. I won't. Instead, I deflect. "How'd you know?"

"Oh, I don't know. It could have been anything from the pink roller skates to the pile of shoes by the door or the fact that you have a stool in your bathroom."

"A stool in my bathroom," I say, raising my brow, suggestively.

"Nice. If there ever is a place to have a stool, the bathroom would be it."

"What?"

I lift my glass from the bar and bring it to my mouth.

"Oh God," she swats at my arm as it dawns on her what I meant. The wine drips a little onto my white shirt. "I don't think I've ever heard a crappier joke. You're terrible."

She has no idea. I like that she's quick. She glances around my living room before looking back at me. "The kids. They're not here, are they?"

"No. Why?"

"We should get to it then."

"Do you do this often?"

She takes the glass from my hand and places it on the bar, moving closer. "Do what often?"

"Go home with men you just met."

"I don't see how that is any of your business," she says, leaning forward, her lips close to my ear.

God, she smells good. "It kind of is."

She steps back and gives me a sideways glance. "Should I go?"

"No," I step forward. "I'm sorry. You're right. It's not my place to ask and—"

"Shhh." She presses her finger to my lips, leaning into me until my back is pressed against the bar. I consider the gun in her purse. I pulled the clip and emptied the chamber. But there are lots of knives in my kitchen.

She pulls my shirt from my waistband and slowly unbuttons it, starting from the top. When she gets to the bottom, I stop her, gripping both her wrists. "What's with the pistol in your purse?"

She squirms, so I tighten my hold. "What?"

"The Glock. Why do you have it?"

Her mouth falls open, but she doesn't look all that surprised. She does, however, give pulling away from me her best effort. "You went through my things?"

"Yes." I put her in a wristlock, which she doesn't take kindly to.

She pushes back, but there's nowhere really for her to go. Her face reddens. "You're hurting me!"

"Tell me why you have the gun," I say, releasing her.

"Why do you think?" She takes three steps backward. Three steps toward the door. "For protection."

Suddenly, the way she says it, it doesn't sound so crazy for a woman with a penchant for one-night stands. Paranoia is something I understand. "I see."

I close the gap between us, grab the back of her neck and pull her into me, kissing her hard on the mouth. She maneuvers out of my grip. "Never ever touch me like you did before. Come at me out of nowhere and you just might get yourself killed."

When I release her, she takes me by the shoulders and spins me around, until I'm facing away from her, toward the kitchen. Then, starting at my ankles, she runs her hands up my thighs and back down again like I'm being frisked and, *oh my God, it's hot and what the fuck is this?*

Her breath is warm on my neck and her hands are everywhere and the next thing I know we're in the kitchen and I'm pinning her to the floor with my knees. She rolls, and I let her until she's on top of me, the look on her face somewhere between desire and murder, and in that moment it doesn't feel like there's a difference and either might be okay.

She leans forward and I sit up, meeting her halfway. She's kissing my neck and my mouth and *fuck*—she's undoing my belt. With a wry grin, she pulls a condom from her bra and holds it up. From there all bets are off. Her clothing goes, along with half of mine, and we are fucking like animals on my kitchen floor. I flip her onto her back.

She begs me not to stop, so I don't. We move to the bedroom where we finish, only to start again. As I dip my tongue inside her, she takes a fistful of my sheets in her fist, ripping them from the corner of the bed. When I plunge deeper, she sucks her lip between her teeth, biting until she draws blood, which I taste when I kiss her. The noises she makes when she is pleased are music to my ears. She's quiet when I'm not quite hitting the mark, but the second I do, she lets out an earth-shattering moan. Ali is a fun instrument to play, the kind you're forever trying to tune, but oh, when you get it right, what a glorious sound she makes.

Fucking her is no different. It's equally fun. She digs her fingernails into my back in a manner that is sure to leave marks, while making the sweetest sounds in my ear—raw, intense, incredible noises, evidence of pure pleasure. She grabs my hair and pulls my head forward as I drive into her. When I hit the spot that turns her moans into one long high-pitch orgasm, she shudders and wraps her quaking legs around me like a boa constrictor entangling its prey. After I finish, I stop to look at her. Her eyes are wild, her hair a tangled mess.

Later, she lays facedown, her left hip curled into my side. "Are you afraid of the dark?"

"What?"

"You have all the lights in the house on. Are you scared of the dark?"

"I don't know." I sigh. "Maybe."

"I like it."

I rest one hand on her thigh. "Do you?"

"Yes," she says. She looks me in the eye. "That way I can see what I'm getting myself into."

"And what's that?"

She smiles. "I haven't decided yet."

CHAPTER TWENTY-ONE

Ethan

Her voice wakes me. It's the sweetest sound you've ever heard, that voice. It calls me from the precipice of sleep with a peaceful resonance, with a sense of ease, with the notion that everything is right in the world. "Hey." I feel her hand on my shoulder. She shakes me gently. "Wake up, sleepy head. Wake up."

From behind my lids, I see golden light. When my eyes flutter open, the room is bathed in it. I cup my hand over my eyes, shielding them. I am not expecting the light to be this intense. "Ah, good. You are alive." *Abby.*

I drop my hand and it hits me the same way it hits me every time I wake. Abby is dead. The palm, resting gently on my shoulder, belongs to the person speaking to me, isn't my daughter.

"Who's Abby?" Ali's voice sounds neutral. Her expression, however, conveys curiosity and if I'm not mistaken, a hint of anger.

"Abby is my daughter. *Was* my daughter."

It rattles me to admit that my daughter is dead, the same way it rattles me every morning when I wake up and the realization hits all over again. The fact that this happens day in and day out does not soften the blow.

"I was dreaming of her I guess." It's been a long time since I've heard Abby's voice in my dreams in a peaceful manner. Most of the time the dream is the same. She screams my name, and when I hear her voice fade there's nothing. Just silence, and a vacant stare attached to her lifeless body. And my hands covered in her blood.

"Abby," Ali says, like she's trying the word out for the first time. "What a beautiful name."

I push myself up to a seated position and reach for my phone. "It's nearly eight."

I never sleep this late. Usually I don't sleep at all.

Ali's hair is wrapped in a towel. Not only has she showered, but she's partially dressed. "How long have you been up?"

"Not long."

"Not long as in five minutes? Or not long as in two hours and you've just been sitting here watching me sleep?"

"Not long as in it's fine."

I reach for her hand but find her wrist. I pull her back into bed. She curls into me, burying her face into my neck. I run my hands up and down the length of her spine, eventually settling at the small of her back.

"Sex first thing is my favorite," she says, lifting her head so that our eyes meet. "Sets you up to win the whole day."

"Are you trying to kill me?"

She offers a suggestive grin. *Damn it*, we went for a triple-header last night. But I suppose I could rally.

"Maybe. Unfortunately, though, I can't stay," she tells me as she practically jumps out of bed. "I have a thing in half an hour." With her hands on her hips, she gives me the once-over. "Rain check?"

I sit up and search the floor for my clothes, then remember they came off in the kitchen. "Let me grab my keys."

"It's okay. I already called for a ride."

"Oh."

"You stay put." She leans down to pat my arm. "I can see myself out."

Throwing the covers off, I plant my feet on the floor and stretch my arms toward the ceiling. "About that rain check."

"I'll call you."

Something in her tone surprises me and I'm almost certain she's lying. "Will you?"

"Maybe."

I follow her down the hall and into the living room, and even though we're in my house, my behavior makes me feel pathetic. Like I'm grasping at something that cannot be held. Ali locates her shoes in the kitchen and quickly slips them on her feet as though hasty exits are a game she's well-versed in. She chews at her lip and knits her brow, making it obvious she's concentrating hard as she searches the living room. She's misplaced something and it gives me an uneasy feeling.

Finally, she shakes her head and lets out a short sigh. "There it is," she says, swiping her purse from the chair.

It's exactly where she left it last night.

"Coffee?"

"Thanks," she tells me with a tight smile. "But my ride's just around the corner."

I realize then that I'm probably not going to see her again. There's always that moment when a woman decides, *this is not for me.* And we've hit that threshold, apparently. What looked good in the dark doesn't appear to be quite as appealing in the light.

"Oh, before I forget." I pull her clip from the drawer where I keep the sandwich bags for the kids' lunches and hold it out to her. As she takes it from my hand, something in her eyes shifts. I can see the barely contained annoyance in them. I'm not sure if it's something I said or if it's always this way with her, but in order to find out I fill the silence. "When's the last time you shot?"

"I don't know," she says in a way that tells me she does know. "It's been a while."

"Yeah, for me, too."

I remove a mug from the cabinet and set it on the counter. "We should go sometime."

She mumbles a yeah or an okay. It's hard to tell because her head is down and she can't take her eyes off her phone. I don't want to feel left out, so I reach for mine. "Sorry." She shakes her head and shifts from one foot to the other. "There's an emergency at work."

I don't respond because whatever I say wouldn't matter. I'm searching for the lid to the coffeepot when I spot the stack of bills laying on the bar, along with papers I emptied from the kids' backpacks but never read. The name on the envelope stares back at me and my breath catches. *Ethan Lane.*

Shit.

"I have to say—" My head jolts up as I hear her click off her phone and set it aside. "I'm a bit surprised. And that doesn't happen too often."

I lean around the bar so I can see her directly. Our eyes meet. "Oh?"

"I really didn't take you for the type of guy who monograms his towels."

Fuck.

"My ex-wife was into that."

A devious expression slides across her face. "I dried myself off with a towel that said E.L. Hopefully, it wasn't hers."

"That's my son's," I say, sliding a flyer for the school carnival over the bills. "Edward. But we call him Nick."

Damn it.

Ali looks somewhere between amused and annoyed.

The first thing about lying if you aren't expecting to is that you have to think quick, and that's usually when you mess up.

Now, I've not only pissed off a potential psychopath, I've given her two of my three children's names, hand delivered her to my home, and if she is the killer, it's possible I've blown my cover completely. But I didn't stop there. I also broke a cardinal rule. Perhaps, *the* cardinal rule. Never have sex with someone who has more to lose than you do.

CHAPTER TWENTY-TWO

Ethan

As I dress for work, it dawns on me that it's Wednesday. My least favorite day of the week, although I suppose waking up with a woman in my bed is an improvement.

Prior to taking the Roberts case, I hated every day equally.

The bright side—at least I get to see the kids.

It's probably better that Ali didn't commit to seeing me again. It's therapy night, which means I get Nick and Kelsey overnight.

Either way, it'd be prudent to put the situation with Ali Brown behind me. While I'm at it I should probably call a realtor. Changing my name, changing *all* of our names for that matter, couldn't hurt. In the event that I have just slept with a serial killer.

The thought gives me a sick feeling in the pit of my stomach. I had the chance once, to do exactly that, to go into WITSEC, the Federal Witness Security Program. If I had been smart enough to take it, life would have turned out very differently.

I picture Ali sitting in that booth at The Crispy Biscuit. I recall her in my bed. I can still smell her in my kitchen. Now, not only do I have the sick feeling in my gut, my chest physically hurts. My mind and my heart do not seem to be playing on the same team.

For a second, I feel a deep sense of longing. It's nice waking up next to someone. I miss that and for a moment, even though Ali may be dangerous, I'm convinced I'm sad about the way things turned out. The way she practically bolted out my front door, without looking back. Not even once.

I realize it's not Ali I'm missing. It's not her I'm sad about.

My emotions are misplaced. There's a term for it in psychology, one I'm sure Ali knows. *Transference.*

I realize that I want to see her again, that I *have* to see her again. Not only do I need to know if she's capable of murder, I need to investigate my feelings. That's what our family therapist constantly tells Bethany and the kids. Me, I refuse to allow Dr. Nancy's lies to reach my ears. Her sing-song voice replays in my mind. *Investigate your feelings, you pussy.* She doesn't put it exactly like that of course, but I know that's what she's thinking. *Man up and deal with it.*

The thought makes the feeling in my stomach worse. God, I hate Wednesdays. I hate therapy. I hate Dr. Nancy. Every week it's the same. Like a sermon on repeat, she preaches about feelings being fleeting, but I know—and Bethany knows—hell, even the kids know—it's all bullshit. There aren't a lot of things I can say with certainty, but the fact that she's full of shit, that, I can say for sure.

Maybe tonight will finally be the night. Maybe tonight when she comes at my family with her psychobabble drivel, I'll do what I've been meaning to do since the first time I stepped foot in her office. I'll ask if she's ever watched her child die. I'll ask if she's ever carefully chosen an outfit for her dead daughter to wear so that her brother and sister can say their goodbyes. I'll ask if she knows how important it is that the clothing be familiar, so she'll look somewhat normal, instead of dead. I'll tell her it's important that they associate their final moments with their sister with positive memories, instead of seeing her for the last time with a bullet hole in her gut, bleeding out all over the living room floor.

Dr. Nancy may know these things in theory but she hasn't lived them. She doesn't have a dead child. So it makes sense that to her, feelings are fleeting. Unfortunately, I won't say any of that. Because the worst part of it? I, too, am full of shit. If I told Dr. Nancy what I really think I'd lose visitation. My weekly visits with my kids are all that I have. That and solving this case.

CHAPTER TWENTY-THREE

Ali

Ali swivels in the high-backed chair and sucks in a deep breath. The lights warm her skin as she counts backward from ten. She feels ready. Expectant. Open. She's supposed to feel gratitude. It isn't easy to land a guest spot on the third top morning show in the country. Not only that, but they slated her interview in the coveted prime-time spot.

She waits for the gratitude to wash over her. Hair and makeup teams have made her look refreshed. Her stylist told her she looks like a million bucks in her black silk suit. Twice.

Ali knows her material. She can recite her answers backward and forward in her sleep. And still she waits for the thankful feeling to hit. Instead, all she feels is the same nagging sense of doubt she gets whenever she speaks in front of people.

She threw up in the green room just seconds before the production assistant came for her. She throws up every time she speaks; it's so bad the acid has rotted out her teeth. Thankfully, veneers and good lighting hide the truth well.

Ali is in good company. They say that public speaking is the second greatest fear people have after dying. But that's not why Ali is afraid. She loves people. She'll have them eating out of her palm in no time. Ali knows that. The producers know that. The host knows that. Half the audience knows that.

But those people aren't what worry Ali. It's the other stuff. Lies that aren't as easy to keep hidden. Lies that have to remain as such.

The lights and the music come up, and it's go-time and Ali smiles for the camera. The host welcomes everyone in and then immediately gets down to business. Airtime is expensive, and she wastes none of it. Sarah Shepard isn't the best. Ali knows this, and Sarah knows this. It's apparent in the set of her jaw as she prattles on and on about Ali's exhaustive list of accomplishments.

Ali smiles proudly but demurely, an expression she's practiced for hours on end in front of the mirror. Facial expressions are important. It's the difference between having someone trust you or not. Ali understands the magic of rapport. She knows words make up only 7 percent of communication. Voice quality makes up 38 percent. But physiology is by far the most important. It can be a matter of life or death. It's not what you say or how you say it, but how you look while you're saying it. A person's physiology makes up 55 percent of what we communicate. Posture, gestures, eye contact, the way you breathe, the way you touch. These things can make or break a situation.

So while what Sarah Shepard is saying sounds good, Ali knows no one really cares. Viewers want confidence and understanding. They want empathy. They want to be armed with the knowledge that will get them what they want. They want her to tell them *what* to do and *how* to do it. They want Ali to get to the point, to the meat of it, which is why at first when she speaks it will be in clipped sentences with a devious grin. She has something they want. And that something is transformation. They want it and they want it yesterday.

Sarah Shepard crosses her legs and gets a look in her eyes that Ali knows well. Sarah sits up a little straighter and goes for the kill. *This is it.* This is the money shot.

"So, Dr. Brown." The camera zooms in on Ali's face. "As a psychologist, I'm sure you've seen a lot."

"People are complex, yes."

"But you deal mainly with complexities related to sex, isn't that right?"

"That's correct."

"What would you tell someone looking to, you know, spice things up in the bedroom?"

Ali smiles bigger this time. She knows how the ball has been teed up. She's seen the interview questions. She knows how she's expected to answer and what limits the network has set. Erectile dysfunction and premature ejaculation, green light. Anal play, menopause, vaginal dryness, off the table. If she can squeeze in the name of a network sponsor, then lube talk is admissible. Kink, unless it alludes to the mention of a certain novel which pays for advertising spots, is also off limits. In that case, it's a gray area, safe when framed right.

Ali squares her shoulders and tilts her head slightly to the right. It's her best angle and it conveys authority. "I would tell them it's important to ask for what they want. Knowing what that is and communicating it in a direct and respectful manner are where a great sex life begins."

The host nods slowly, like she's taking it all in. Like Ali's answer was the only probable response she could have given. "Don't you think it's important to have that conversation—or at least to start it—outside of the bedroom?"

"It's *very* important. Most things in relation to sex start outside the bedroom."

Sarah Shepard smoothed her red hair, flipping it off her shoulder. The gesture and hair color make Ali think of her father, or rather the man who called himself that. The man who raised her. He hated redheads. He always said that if Ali had been a redhead, he would have left her at the hospital. At nine, Ali saved her three months of allowance for hair dye. She believed that if she changed herself into something he despised, he would leave her alone. Turned out, that was just another of his lies.

"Easy for you to say, looking like that," Sarah motions. "But what do you say to all the women out there watching who don't have hair and makeup teams to make them look like you do? What do you say to all the exhausted moms watching in sweatpants while folding laundry?"

Ali swallows. This isn't a question that was on the list. "I tell them to take a shower and greet their partner at the door. Maybe skip the drying off part. To save time."

"But you said it starts outside the bedroom."

Ali nods. "Exactly."

When the canned laughter fades, Sarah Shepard changes direction. "You're known for using less conventional methods of teaching your clients about sex, aren't you, Dr. Brown?"

This question was also not on the interview sheet. Ali shoots her shot anyway. "Convention can be hard to define," she says. "And it's different around the world." Ali smiles for the camera, but she knows what she's saying isn't true. Convention in public is very easy to define. Behind closed doors, not so much.

"How would you say it's different? Around the world."

Sarah Shepard wants her to pit certain countries against one another, making one good, the other bad. Ali refuses the bait. "There are certain parts of the world that are more open toward sex, where it's talked about a little more freely."

"In the Western world that's not the case though, is it?"

"We talk about it in different ways. Through art and film, for example. But not so much directly, yes."

"In your seminars you're well-known for simulating sex with

fruit." The host turns and watches the screen behind her where a clip of Ali presenting *Foreplay is f*king fun* plays.

In the clip, played solely for the studio audience, a volunteer at one of her seminars simulates oral sex with a banana. The camera records the reactions of the audience, flashing from person to person as they laugh and shake their heads. Some look away. Those who don't, their eyes widen as the clip pans to a shot of Ali using grapefruit to show ways to please a woman.

"It works," Ali says with a shrug when the clip finishes. "As you can see."

"What would you say about gender fluidity, Dr. Brown?" Sarah Shepard cocks her head and goes further off-script. "Most of your material is geared toward heterosexual men and women. But what about people that fall outside of the so-called—" she pauses and makes air quotes "—norm?"

Ali recognizes what Sarah is doing, but she can't very well stop it now. "Genitals are mostly the same, no matter how a person identifies. It's only the language that changes."

"So are you denying that maybe your work is not as progressive as it could be?"

"My work helps people have more fulfilling sex lives. My only agenda is to help people feel better."

"But they can't feel better if they don't feel accepted, isn't that right?"

"Of course. I see clients in my personal practice that are grappling with a variety of issues."

"And yet in your seminars you still use outdated terminology to describe male and female anatomy?"

"I wouldn't call it outdated. It's scientific. It's anatomy and physiology 101."

"Science changes though, doesn't it, Dr. Brown?" She turns to the camera, but she speaks to Ali. "Can you imagine if we still taught our doctors some of the practices that physicians learned a century ago?"

Ali hates being ambushed, and this is exactly what this is. "Sex is still sex. My mission is the same as it has always been. To help people—*all people*—anyone who *wants* help. My goal is to help them find pleasure and to be open and honest about how it happens. But it's fair to say that some people don't want help, Sarah. And those people, they like to complain. But rarely does casual effort provide extraordinary results."

"Let's shift gears," Sarah Shepard says, and the camera pans out. "What would you say brought on this obsession with sex? Were you interested from a very young age?" She touches her face and her expression morphs into a sort of mixed curiosity. Ali can see that Ms. Shepard has also perfected her facial expressions. "Tell us. What brings one to this line of work?"

Ali smiles because she understands what is happening. This interview is not about her. It's not about ratings. It's about advertising dollars. And the best way to get ratings? Controversy.

"Like I said, I've always wanted to make people happy. And sex has always been this sort of taboo topic that leads to a lot of pain. But underneath that is shame."

"Shame. It's interesting that you bring that word up. Do you think your chosen career path has anything to do with your past?"

Ali thinks Sarah Shepard is about to grasp at straws and ask if she's sexually fulfilled. It won't be the first time an interview or a fan has demanded answers about her personal life. But that's not what happens at all. "Your father," Sarah says, pointing at her notes. "He molested you. Surely that has had an immense effect on your work."

Ali feels her face grow hot. The lights are suddenly burning holes in her skin. "No," she shakes her head. "You must be mistaken."

"That's interesting." The host double checks her notes. "I'm sorry. Somehow my producers must have gotten that wrong." She seems flustered, but Ali knows it's an act. "You work with a lot of victims of sexual abuse. Maybe it was implied—"

"Through my foundation, yes."

"Incredible work you do there." A promotional clip plays on the screen of Ali in jeans and a T-shirt working with human trafficking victims.

"Do you have anything you'd like to say? I mean, if someone out there who is a survivor—or worse—is currently in a situation where they are being abused, and they're watching, what would you say to them?"

Ali sits up a little straighter and the camera moves in close on her face. "I would tell them they are not a product of their circumstances—that the abuse is not their fault and that it's important to talk to a trained professional. But most importantly, they need to make sure they're safe. It's vital they make plans to get out of their situation, as difficult as that may seem. It's possible. I've worked with thousands of survivors of abuse."

The outro music starts and the lights go up. "Well, you've certainly done exactly that. Everyone, let's give it up for Dr. Ali Brown!"

Canned applause cues up. "Thank you for being with us today, Dr. Brown."

CHAPTER TWENTY-FOUR

I t's hard to prove a murder when you don't have a body. Damn near impossible. So when I kidnap *the* Sarah Shepard, the nasally talk show host? I'm not exactly—how do you say—trying to keep her around. Trust me, no one wants a woman like that. Sarah Shepard is the stench of reality in your nose: the hard facts, the lessons you didn't want to learn. It takes a lot of mental energy trying to figure out what to do with her. Too bad employers aren't interested in people with a knack for that. It ought to be a desirable skill set, the kind you could somehow work into a resume. *Excels at knowing how to make a person disappear.*

Alas, Sarah Shepard will not be found. She was a problem, and I am what you could call a problem solver. Like a lot of women in her profession, Sarah was a workaholic and a fitness fanatic. I couldn't exactly go for her at the station. Lights, camera, action, and all. Good thing she liked to jog. Alone. On rural roads. With earbuds in. Not the brightest. But I didn't want to go the hit-and-run route. I really like my car.

So I took a chance and asked for help. And, well, if you know anything about murder, then you know this is usually where the real problems start.

CHAPTER TWENTY-FIVE

Ethan

Nadia is positively glowing when I walk through the door. She hands me a cup of coffee, wearing a smile the likes of which I have never seen. It's certainly not her typical greeting. I can't say I'm surprised given the morning I've had. I'm not exactly batting a thousand where women are concerned.

"Morning, boss." Her brow is raised, and her grin is so wide I can see her gums. Nadia is not big on smiles. "Camille Roberts is in your office."

And there it is. "Don't call me boss. Just Ethan will do."

"Okay, 'Just Ethan,' whatever floats your boat."

I give her a sideways glance.

"Oh, and good news!" She raises her mug in cheers. "We still have internet."

"She doesn't have an appointment."

"I said that, boss. I tried. I really did. But you know *her*. She told me—with a flick of her perfect wrist and her perfectly mani-cured fingers—to go fuck myself."

My jaw tenses. "Sounds like Camille."

"Doesn't it? What can I say? A vagina combined with an atti-tude is a lethal combination."

"I just can't imagine how she couldn't win over the detectives working her father's case."

Nadia shrugs. "Your guess is as good as mine."

"Did you bring the file?"

"The file?"

"From Max."

Her brows shoot up and she holds up her index finger. "Um…" She reaches down and pulls it slyly from her desk drawer. "Gotcha! Of course I did. And it's good, boss. It's very good."

"How many times have I told you? Stop calling me boss. You know I hate that." I glance toward my office and then back at Nadia. "Wait. How good?"

She nods vigorously. Camille's visits really light her up. She'll never admit it, but Nadia aspires to be exactly like Camille. "Juicy good."

"That *is* good."

"Lucas Bennett kept a journal."

I let out a deep exhale. I might just solve this case after all. "Great," I flip through the file. "Let me deal with *her* and we'll sit down and take a look."

"Good luck," Nadia says, reaching for the manila folder. "You're going to need it. She's in a special mood today."

I keep the file just out of her reach. "Special mood?" My eyes widen. "What does that mean? Give it to me in male terms."

"You'll see."

I glance toward my office. Camille is sitting in the chair behind my desk, *my* chair. She folds her arms across her chest and glares at me with a barely contained rage. A little wave is all it takes for her to lose it. She jumps to her feet, which is impressive

KILL ME TOMORROW: A PSYCHOLOGICAL THRILLER

in six-inch heels, and gestures dramatically at her Rolex, stabbing at it with her index finger.

"Fucking rich people," Nadia says. "So impatient."

"Time is money and money is time," I tell her, chugging my coffee. I'm almost grateful it has long gone cold. "Make sure she gets billed from the second she stepped through the door until the second she steps out. If I'd known she was here, I would've circled the block a few times."

"If you'd known," Nadia says. "You wouldn't have showed at all."

"I'M GOING TO NEED A SECOND," I SAY, SINKING DOWN INTO MY chair. I'm careful not to make eye contact as I lean forward and move several items around my desk, only to move them right back. "You don't have an appointment. Remember? We talked about that."

I feel her eyes burning holes in me as I type in my password and click a few tabs open. She scoffs and paces my office. Camille is the type of woman who commands an audience and won't settle for anything less. When I'm satisfied, I look up and meet her. "Ms. Roberts." I lift my pen and doodle on the yellow tablet in front of me. "Tell me, to what do I owe the pleasure of your presence?"

"Cut the shit, Lane." She takes three steps toward me and yanks the pen from my hand. She drops it onto the desk, just out of my reach. "You know neither of us enjoy the fact that I'm here."

She continues to pace the small office. It's much too early for that kind of fervor. Camille's known to be a fan of the white stuff, and it looks like she's had a few bumps already this morning.

She stops, whips her head around, and gives me the once-over. "You know I hate it when you call me that," she seethes. "My name is *Camille*. Roberts was my—" She pauses and looks at me with her mouth gaping open. She's lost her train of thought midsentence.

Usually coke heightens a person's cognitive abilities. Her coke habit seems to have the opposite effect. She's not making any sense. She recovers, though. "That was my father's name. You may refer to me by my first name."

"Of course." Camille is not a feminist. If she were, she wouldn't be in my office desperate to get her hands on money she didn't earn.

"Speaking of my father—"

Camille has come for her weekly progress update. Uninvited. As usual. "I said I'd call with any news. I say that every week. And yet here you are."

"And yet here I am."

"Good. Because since you're here you should know I'm making progress."

She tilts her head to the side. "What kind of progress are we talking? Because last I checked, my father is still dead, and no one has been arrested for his MURDER!"

"Don't scream, Camille."

She looks at me like she's a child whose just been scolded. A child who doesn't think they've done anything wrong.

"Do you have any idea—any idea whatsoever—how humiliating this is? Do you have any idea what people are saying? The lies!"

"I can only imagine."

She transforms before my eyes from angry Camille into a whiny, malevolent version of herself. This one is extra. Extra hard to get rid of. "People think Daddy had some weird sex fetish."

"The term you're looking for is erotic asphyxiation. And maybe he did."

"Don't be ridiculous."

I almost tell her that a thirty-something-year-old woman calling their father Daddy is the ridiculous part, but I don't want to kick a hornet's nest. Instead I say, "Sometimes we don't know people the way we think we do."

"I know my father. And I know that my father would never in a million years kill himself."

Her opinion makes me think of Kelsey. I wonder if she might someday say the same.

The TV in the waiting area flashes. I catch it from the corner of my eye. Camille follows my gaze. "Oh God, not her again."

Ali Brown fills the screen. I can't hear what is being said, not with the glass wall between me and the television. But I can read body language and hers doesn't look good. The ticker across the bottom reads *sex therapist helps victims of sexual abuse.* "You know her?"

"Of course I know her," Camille spits. "Everyone knows her."

She leans on the corner of my desk and watches the TV, shaking her head. "Daddy was a big fan. Me, not so much."

"My ex-wife, too." The jury is still out on how I feel, but this, I keep to myself.

"Funny thing though. She's just like every other so-called expert."

"How's that?"

Camille Roberts rolls her eyes. "She's full of shit."

CHAPTER TWENTY-SIX

Ethan

I'm still at my desk long after the sun has gone down. The office is dark and eerily quiet, the way I like it. Nadia left hours ago, and while I could do the same thing I'm doing here from my home office, there's something about going home to an empty house I just can't face.

Two days have passed since Camille Roberts showed up in my office, and while I've made several calls resulting in me making some headway on the case, it hasn't been much. Other work has superseded it. Other rabbit holes have demanded my attention. Rabbit holes that have easier answers and instant gratification.

I flip on the lamp on my desk only to turn it off again. Using just the glow of my computer screen, I pick up the file on the senator's kid, Lucas Bennett, and shuffle through it again, waiting for something to grab me.

Somewhere down the hall, I hear the steady hum of a vacuum cleaner. I close the file and stare at the wall. The paint is called

Network Gray. I hate it. I've always hated it. It was Bethany's choice, like most everything else in this place.

The file on my desk beckons me to pick it up. It screams *read me again,* and I wonder what I might find if I dig deep enough. I know all too well about coming up with more than you went in for. Knowledge hurts people. There's a saying that comes from the Alcoholics Anonymous world, that you're only as sick as your secrets.

If a person has secrets, or even unfulfilled desires, and that person is hiding those from other people, they're suppressing what they want and that makes them sick. The pain of suppression usually starts small, like a whisper. But over time, like anything, if it's ignored, that whisper grows louder and louder, demanding more and more attention. Until it becomes too much and they find a way to meet that need.

I think of Lucas Bennett and try to put myself in his shoes. It's not hard. I've been there. Sometimes I'm still there. I know what it's like to carry the weight of the ever present, soul-crushing, gut-wrenching reality that you just don't want to be alive anymore. I know what it's like to not to want to exist, sitting day in and day out, listening to the sounds that only an empty house can make. Or hanging out in a dark office that's painted a color you don't even like, waiting for your phone to ring, or for a response on an app, just so you don't have to go home alone, or sit alone with yourself any longer. That's not living. It's going through the motions with working lungs and a heart that continues to beat. It's a sick and cruel form of punishment.

Sometimes I sit in therapy and I ponder the number of times I'll see the furrow of Nick's brow or the curve of Kelsey's smile and I tell myself, maybe next week. Maybe next week I'll get the guts.

Back when Bethany and I were still married, I mentioned having suicidal thoughts. I was worried I might actually act on them, and although I never would have admitted it at the time, in a way it was a call for help.

"And so why haven't you done it, Ethan?" Bethany said when I told her how I'd been feeling. "Why haven't you killed yourself?" We were fighting over the tile selection for the employee restroom and it just hit me. Enough was enough. I didn't care about tile. I didn't care about anything. I didn't have an answer for her then. Back when it might have mattered. But I do now.

I refuse to leave my children the way my father left me, alone with my mother, desolate and filled with grief. It wasn't the fact that he left, that one day he went out for cigarettes and never came back. That was the good part. It just would've been better if we hadn't been constantly broke. Proving that Donovan Roberts was murdered will allow me to leave my children a nest egg behind, which is why I have to be careful. If I die before that happens, they get nothing.

Of course, I'd have to make it look like an accident. Or murder. Shouldn't be too hard. This case is certainly teaching me the ins and outs of getting a proper pay out.

My phone lights up and I snatch it from the desk as though it may grow legs and run off. I wouldn't be surprised. Everything else in my life has. I read the notification, which turns out to be from Apple, suggested tips on how to take better photos, capturing more details at night. If I hadn't felt shitty enough before, I certainly do now.

Ali is never going to call. Denial runs deep. But it doesn't run deep enough to silence that little voice inside that keeps telling you you're missing an unpleasant truth.

I've sent Ali two messages from inside the app. I'd call her, or text, but I can't let on that I have her phone number because I never actually asked her for it. You can find anything on the internet. But I need to be subtle. I don't want to scare her off any more than I probably already have. Both messages in the app went unread. Not that I hadn't expected that, but it still sucks. No one wants to be rejected, apparently not even by a possible serial killer.

Sure, I'd like to sleep with her again, but I also have other motives. Lucas Bennett's journal entries indicate he might have dated Ali. There are certain behavioral similarities between what he described and my experience with her. Using an alias. Turning up unexpectedly. The sudden mood shift. The walking out abruptly.

His journal made him sound sad and lonely at times. Not atypical for an artist type. He described periods of feeling high and low. He wrote he felt like he was getting nowhere. Nothing too out of the ordinary for a young man his age. If he wanted to end his life, he certainly didn't leave any clues about it. But who is to say how a person really feels inside? I know his journal was just a glimpse in time. A snapshot of a moment. To understand more, I'd have to speak with those closest to him and I can't get around to that until next week. I have the kids this weekend.

For now, I have three main questions: Does Ali Brown have a type? It seems that she might. Should I be scared? Probably. Am I scared? A little.

It's not a bad thing. Fear is always informing you. Although surely if she were planning to kill me, she would have responded to my direct messages or at least shown some level of interest. Otherwise, what's in it for her? Why would she wait? Also, it seems very unlikely that she would go after someone so high profile, like a senator's kid. Unless, of course, she didn't know.

CHAPTER TWENTY-SEVEN

Ethan

Here's a lesson for everyone. Never give up. Ten minutes later, ten minutes after I told myself it was *never* going to happen, a notification from the app came in. I have three messages, two from women I've matched with, and the only one I really want, a message from Ali.

She apologizes and says she's had to take an emergency trip out of town for work, but that she has a gift for me and could I go to this address tonight, as in the next half hour. It sounds like a terrible idea. I jot down the address and then look it up. It takes me to the Circuit of The Americas, the Formula One racetrack just outside of town. *When you get there,* she wrote, *ask for Chris. Tell him Ali sent you. He'll be expecting you. He'll be expecting me too. Just explain about the last-minute emergency trip. Act really sorry, and it'll probably work.*

I check the time on my phone. The map app says it'll take me twenty-eight minutes to get there from my office. If this is how she's planning to kill me, I don't care. I'll give her an A for effort. It's one way I hadn't thought of myself.

THIS IS RACING SCHOOL, CHRIS EXPLAINS TO ME. HE'S A HANDSOME fellow, tall and tanned, the kind of man you'd be sorry for the lady in your life to know. It's too late for that, but I keep a close eye on him, anyway. I wonder if he's slept with her. When I ask how he knows Ali, he only smiles and changes the subject, and I pretty much have my answer. Not only that, if he's doing this kind of favor, he's in deep. But at least he isn't dead.

Chris hands me a suit and a helmet, a pen, and a very long waiver with lots of fine print. It's all wasted ink. I would have signed it in blood.

The track at night is really something. It's all lit up and empty. It smells like fuel and burnt rubber and the scent of tires long after they've struck the asphalt. "This is amazing," I say as he directs me toward the passenger seat of the car. Not only has he slept with the woman of my dreams, he's about to show me he's an incredible driver too. He looks over at me from the driver's seat and smiles. "You ready? I'm going to show you what an automobile is capable of doing."

That's the last thing I hear before I am slammed back into the seat. We're going one hundred and fifty miles an hour straight at a wall into a hairpin turn. Next are the corkscrew turns and my heart is about to beat out of my chest. The entire ride has my hair on end. I know, without a doubt, the car is going to flip. We're going to wipe out.

After the fourth hairpin turn, I realize then what Ali's done. Her gift is not just about the racetrack. It's a great metaphor. Everyone likes when they're in control. If you're on a motorcycle and you're in front *and* you know what you're doing, then you're

KILL ME TOMORROW: A PSYCHOLOGICAL THRILLER

relatively comfortable. But if you're on the back, it's an entirely different ride.

Ali sent me a follow-up message before I got here that didn't make a lot of sense then, but it does now. She said this is how most people live their life. It's like they're on the back of the motorcycle and on the front is all the demands in their life. That's who's driving—all the things they're afraid of, all the things other people want from them, all the things they'd like to do right now. The problem is they don't really know what to do to make those things happen. So they get whipped around.

When Chris is done with the ride, he pulls over. I've just gotten whipped around. My heart is still pounding when he turns to me and says, "In two days' time, you'll be doing this too."

I think, *yeah right*. I think, *there isn't anything I'd rather be doing*. I think, *I'm going to die*. I think, *so what?*

Chris looks serious. "There's one thing you need to know to be really good. In order to be a good driver, there's one skill above all else. And if you don't get it, you're going to crash and burn."

"What's that?"

"You must learn how to come out of a spin."

"Come out of a spin. Okay."

"Because what'll happen is you'll be driving along and even if you're doing everything right, somebody else is going to screw up and it's going to affect you. They're going to break up in front of you and you're going to have to figure out how to get around it. Or there will be oil up ahead that's slick and you won't see it and you'll spin out of control."

"Spin out of control. Right." I had a hard time keeping up with him. He talks as fast as he drives.

"You have to figure out how to turn it around."

I nod. He looks at me as though what he's saying might be going in one ear and out the other. Like he's been talking to my ex-wife.

"You can't merely react. You have to be in charge."

"Got it. Be in charge."

"Look, if you're going to be successful as a driver, you've got to come out of the spin and I'm going to show you how it works. I'm going to put you in a spin car."

Chris extricates himself from the car and helps me out. He heads toward the building and gestures for me to follow.

He opens the garage door and shows me another car inside. It looks beat to hell. "Sit down in this thing," he tells me, holding the door open. "Look what I've got in my hand here."

He showed me a small device with four buttons.

"Four buttons," I say blankly. "What do they do?"

He shoves it closer. I feel the color drain from my face. I'm hoping he's not going to blow the car up. "So when we're driving, at any moment, I can push any one of these four buttons and it will lift the wheel that relates to that part of the car and we will spin out of control in that direction."

Is he for real? Forty-five minutes ago I was sitting alone in my dark office thinking of different ways to kill myself and now this.

"I'm not going to push the button when you're ready for it. I'm not going to make it convenient. Because that's not how it works in racing. You're not ready when it happens to you. You're never ready."

He climbs in the passenger seat after strapping me in the harness and we drive. I go around and around the track. At least twenty times. I'm thinking, *okay I'm ready*. Go ahead and push the button. But then I remember he hasn't actually told me what I'm supposed to do when he pushes it. And when I look over at him, he's grinning because he realizes this too.

I slow the car and say, "What do I do when I get caught in the spin?"

He nods proudly. "There's only one thing you have to remember. Focus on where you want to go and steer that way."

"Steer that way," I repeat.

"What are you most afraid of?"

"Dying?"

"You're most afraid of hitting the wall."

"Right."

"Don't focus on what you fear. You know where all the walls are. If you look at what you're afraid of, you'll literally steer into it."

"Don't look at the walls."

"You're going to be driving incredibly fast and I'm going to push the button and you're going to spin out of control and your first instinct is to go looking for the wall to see where it is. But if you look toward the wall, you're going to steer us into it, and you can literally get us killed. So I'm going to be here to make sure you focus."

"Great." My heart is pounding out of my chest. I don't think I've ever felt more alive.

I speed up and after two-and-a-half laps, he pushes the button.

"Get away from the wall by turning to the left!" he yells.

He forces my head left, making me look that way. But there's lag time. Momentum. I'm not expecting that. He keeps forcing my face left. Eventually the wheels catch.

Second time around, I immediately look at the wall. I want to see death when it comes. He forces my head left. At the last second, the wheels catch.

It takes me six tries before I immediately stop looking for the wall. "You have to build the response into your nervous system," Chris says. "But if you look at what you're afraid of, you're going to drive right into it."

CHAPTER TWENTY-EIGHT

Ethan

Drizzle falls from the dark sky. A storm is rolling in fast. I hear thunder booming in the distance. It's late when I pull into my drive. I'm still high from my experience at the racetrack. Large drops pelt my windshield, a welcome sight. The mixture of adrenaline and the usual insomnia make me grateful for the rain. It's a peaceful distraction. There are just a few hours before I have to be up.

I sit in my car for a bit watching the rain and before I know it, the rush of the racetrack subsides and I start to dread going inside. I think about the past and wonder how I ended up in this situation. In a rundown house, in a rundown neighborhood. It was never meant to be permanent. After Bethany confessed her love for someone else, I moved out. I found this house and made an offer on a whim. I had planned on fixing it up and flipping it. Yet, here I am two years later.

When I press the button to lift the garage door, nothing

happens. The battery must have gone out or a spring broke. Either way, it's always something with this house. I pull the key from the ignition, leave the car in the driveway, and start up the walk. I tell myself when I get inside I'll check the weather app to see if hail is in the forecast.

The low clouds are suffocating as I make my way toward the front door. The familiar lump in my throat I get every time I come home and the house is empty makes itself known. I'm greeted by a pitch black porch. The porch light is off or out. I can't recall if I flicked it on this morning. Before sticking the key in the lock, I use the flashlight on my phone to take a peek at the bulb. It could be out. It often stays on for days. I usually enter through the garage.

My fingers graze the smooth metal of my handgun as I slide my hand along the holster attached to my belt. When I contact the rough texture of the handle, I exhale slowly. My anxiety coupled with my training make me register details other people might not. In law enforcement, you never really turn off. The smallest details are noted and catalogued. Like the fact that Mr. Stevens has three newspapers scattered across his driveway. *Is he out of town? Sick? In the hospital?* And the Jacobs family? They have two cars parked at the curb in front of their house. Cars that aren't usually there. *Are they visitors or something more sinister?* I try to recall whether I've seen them before and can't. I do my best not to spend a lot of time at home.

Turning the key in the lock, I keep one hand at my hip, on my gun, while the other twists the door handle. I fling the door open wide and lean in and flip the light switch at the door, illuminating the living area. I forgot to close the blinds in the back before I left. My reflection in the glass stares back at me. I look ridiculous, wide-eyed and on edge, in the ready stance.

I close the door. After locking the deadbolt, I set the chain and then punch in the code for the alarm. Thunder booms like a bowling ball rolling through an air duct. It's louder this time, and the sky outside flashes bright. Once, twice, three times. I wait for the thunder to follow, counting down.

After tossing my keys into the bowl on the counter, I shrug out of my suit jacket and sling it over the couch. I stop abruptly when the floor creaks down the hallway. There's a burning sensation at my neck, like someone's watching me, and I know I'm not alone. I draw my weapon and duck into the kitchen, putting a wall between me and the intruder. I flip the safety and chamber a round.

"Jesus," a distinctly female voice groans. "I give you a gift. It's like you're not grateful at all."

Ali's tone is amused. It's playful and slightly annoyed. When I round the corner, weapon drawn, she stands there glaring at me, stark naked. In one hand she holds a bottle of champagne. The other is on her hip. She looks at me with a hunger that makes my stomach flutter with fear. "I thought we could celebrate your first lesson."

"I thought you were out of town," I say, although this isn't the first question to come to mind. *Is she alone? How did she get in here? Is she fucking crazy?*

"I will be soon." She smiles and tucks a stray lock of hair behind her ear with her free hand. "I wanted to leave you with a parting gift. I missed you."

I don't believe her, but with hips and tits like that, it's hard to turn down a gift. She looks incredible, so fucking incredible, that I don't think I could say no, even if I wanted to. "You do realize you're breaking and entering and I could shoot you no problem."

"Trust me," she says. "It would be a very big problem."

"Is this what you do?" I train my gun on her. "Just turn up?"

"How else is it supposed to be a surprise?"

"We've only been on one date. Showing up at my house seems a little premature." I glance around the place. "How'd you get in?" I ask. The alarm was set. The doors were locked. I'm not exactly a novice when it comes to home security.

"The other night when you brought me home, I watched you type in the code."

"And?"

She gives a sly smile. "And…I might've copied your key."

"You copied my house key?"

"They have kits for that, you know. Online. You can find almost anything."

"What—while I was sleeping?"

She shrugs. "Well, it sure wasn't while we were fucking."

The necklace that falls between her perfect breasts catches my eye, the diamond moving in time with her increased heart rate.

I've never met anyone like her. And I don't think I ever will again. "You're fucking insane."

"You have no idea."

I might. "So what now?"

"First, you put down the gun. And then we toast to your first lesson."

"My lesson? Racing school?" I ask, swallowing hard.

She tilts her head and raises one brow suggestively. "I haven't decided yet."

WE MOVE TOWARD THE BEDROOM, MY PISTOL AIMED AT HER BACK. I wonder what kind of good defense you'd need to get away with shooting a naked woman in your house. Especially one you've dated. It sounds expensive. I wonder what prison is like and it isn't looking good.

I follow her slowly, feeling like I'm being lured into a trap, as though a way out is slowly closing, cutting off my escape route entirely.

If the sight of her from behind is any indication of what's coming, I'm not sure I mind.

We reach my bedroom, which is lit up by dozens of candles. I can't know for sure whether it's romantic or whether a human sacrifice is about to take place. On my nightstand sit two champagne flutes. Ali shifts and turns abruptly, placing her hand on the gun. "I don't mind a little kink." She fingers the tip. "But this is a bit much, don't you think?"

She drops her hand and holds up the champagne bottle. Once I've placed my gun back in the holster, she thrusts the bottle in my direction. "You do the honors."

"I'm not in the mood for a drink."

"So? Get in the mood. Moods are choices, you know."

I pop the bottle and watch as the bubbly liquid spills over the sides. It runs down my hand and trickles onto the floor. She takes the bottle from me, and then takes my hand in hers, bringing my hand to her mouth. Suggestively, she sucks the champagne off my fingers. I can't tell if she's serious, but it certainly feels that way. "I know you're not an attorney—" she says, dropping my hand. "Or an accountant or whatever bullshit you said. And I know your name isn't Mark."

"You broke into my house. Obviously, you know a lot of things."

"I'm very resourceful, Ethan. Very, *very* resourceful."

"I have no doubt."

"What I want to know is what you know about me?" she asks, turning on her heel. She walks on tiptoe toward the bed, stopping to stretch her arms toward the ceiling, arching her back in a way that makes me dizzy. Then she drops back on to the mattress, calling me with her finger as she slowly spreads her legs wide open.

My eyes widen. "You're not great at television interviews. I know that."

"Oh, Ethan, Ethan, Ethan, Ethan. That wasn't an interview. That was an ambush."

The way she says my name is hypnotizing. She pops one finger in her mouth and starts sliding it down her body, and then—

"Come here," she says.

I follow her direction. "God," she murmurs, as my mouth moves from one breast to the other. She arches her back again as two of my fingers work inside her. It's a tight fit, but nothing she can't handle. When I add my thumb, pressing it against her clit, her eyes roll back in her head. She squirms, but I don't stop. I keep working her over. I let her get close, so close. Then I stop and pull away.

"What are you doing?"

"You seem to like lessons," I shrug. "Figure it out."

She looks at me incredulously at first and then with an intense defiance. "Fine."

I can't look away. Especially not when she replaces my fingers with hers. She knows exactly what to do, and I am blessed with a front row seat. The strength of what she's building is staggering. Fascinating. Breathtaking. And I can't let her go it alone. I yank my jeans off, take two quick steps toward the bed, towering over her. She doesn't stop, so I take her hands and pin them behind her head. Then I position myself just right, plunging into her fast. When she digs her nails into my wrist, I stop and go slow. Painfully slow.

"Please," she cries.

I tighten my grip on her wrists. Squeezing hard enough that she's forced to draw back on her nails digging into my skin.

"Do it," she whispers into my ear. "I know where your children go to school."

I almost pause. Almost. But not quite. She's fucking crazy, and the only thing you can do with crazy is to meet it where it is. And then take it a bit further. Switching positions, I take both her wrists in one hand, and cup my other hand over her mouth, using my thumb and forefinger to pinch off the air supply to her nose.

"You may know my name and you may know where I live. But you don't know me like you think you do."

The color drains from her face as she strains against my hand, twisting her face from side to side. I speed up. Thrusting harder and faster.

When I eventually let go and release her nose, she gasps, sucking in a deep breath. I slow again. "If you stop, I'll kill you," she says. And I believe her.

She comes groaning, every muscle in her body drawn taut.

I follow suit.

Then I collapse into her and we lay there, eyes wide open, listening to the storm rage outside. Neither of us speaks. Lightning flashes across the walls at regular intervals. At some point I fall asleep.

I wake shortly before the sun is up, but she's already gone.

CHAPTER TWENTY-NINE

Ali

Seattle

Everyone has a plan until they get hit in the face. Ali will tell you it was Mike Tyson who said that. She'll also tell you it's true. She's been hit in the face enough times to know.

"I know what you're up to." David had texted her at 3 a.m. It's not the kind of message a woman wants to receive from their new fiancé. "I know what kind of person you are."

As it turns out, David's mother is Sarah Shepard's number one fan, and after Ali's less than stellar interview with the morning show anchor, David's mother noticed that one Dr. Ali Brown looks a lot like her son's new fiancée, also named Sarah. David realized this too, once his mother so kindly brought it to his attention, and then David wondered what else Ali had been lying about. He didn't just wonder. He did a bit of digging.

Ali sighed. Knowing what's coming when she lands makes for a very long flight from Austin to Seattle. Ali doesn't know what she's going to find when she gets there, something that both terrifies and excites her.

There are only a few ways things can go when the man who asked you to marry him a little over a week ago realizes that not only are you *not* who you told him you were, but you've also been logging into his bank account over the last five weeks, slowly siphoning money into an offshore account. It's not like it was a lot of money. Nothing that would send red flags. Nothing that can't be replaced. Nothing that might tie Ali to the transfers.

Unless, of course, her lovely fiancé planted a camera in his home office and caught her in the act. Which he did. Or so he says. Either way, she's in trouble plenty.

Not only has she stolen from him, she's humiliated him. She knows from their conversations over the last six weeks that humiliation is his biggest fear. On one hand, this made him easy to seduce. She leaned into that fear, played it like a fiddle. On the other hand, trust once broken can scarcely be regained. Ali knows this relationship is over. She just has to bring it to a close smoothly, or as smoothly as possible, all things considered. She needs to end it in a way that won't make things worse for her.

She fishes the engagement ring from her carry-on and slips it on her finger, holding her hand at arm's length to admire the clarity of the diamond.

It's such a shame things had to end this way. David is a nice guy. He is decent in bed. He will make a good husband to someone. Just not her.

ALI ISN'T SURE WHAT TO EXPECT WHEN SHE KNOCKS ON THE DOOR of David's condo. Usually she lets herself in, but she knows this visit is different. It's important that she convey respect. It's vital that she shows she understands the seriousness and the severity of what she's done.

She knocks twice and waits for several minutes, although he's expecting her. She had texted him from the car. He answers the door, looking like a shell of himself. He's disheveled, looking like he hasn't slept in days.

This is all it takes for Ali to realize just how much trouble she's in. David is a large man, much larger and stronger than she is. She has to be careful. She has to play her cards just right. Cornering a wounded animal is dangerous.

David leaves the door open and walks away, forcing her to close it behind her.

He slinks down on the couch, which faces his multi-million-dollar view of Puget Sound. He stares straight ahead, but not at the gorgeous view. His eyes are fixed on a spot on the wall. She stands in the entryway considering whether or not to enter, or to turn and go. She wonders how long he's known.

"David? Are you okay?" she asks quietly. She takes a few cautious steps in his direction.

His head whips up. "Does it look like I'm okay?"

There's anger in his tone and a little venom, and sadness in his eyes. Ali knows this is a worst-case scenario. Anger, she can soothe. But when sadness takes its grip, all bets are off. "I know you're angry and I'm sorry."

"Are you, Sarah? I mean, *Ali*? Are you *really*?"

"If I weren't, I wouldn't have come."

"I could ruin you, you know."

"Yes," she says. "I lied to you and you'd have every right."

He isn't expecting her to say this, but he isn't buying it, either.

"You know the really fucked up part? If you'd just have asked for the money, I'd have given it to you."

Ali knows this is at least partially a lie. He might have given it to her, but he would have lost respect for her for asking. It would have been the beginning of the end, the same as her stealing it.

"I know." She perches on the edge of his sofa. Close, but not too close. "And I should have asked. But I was embarrassed."

"You don't have it in you to be embarrassed. You're not that kind of woman."

She swallows and looks away, toward the trees and the water. There's a long silence. She's going to miss this view.

"What'd you do with it, anyway?"

"I paid my father off."

"Your father? I thought you said your parents were dead."

"There are different kinds of dead."

He stands and crosses the living room. It's an open floor plan, which makes it hard to tell where he's going. Eventually, he sits at the piano. He strokes a few keys, hitting all the sad notes.

"I can repay you. I just need a little time." This is a lie, but sometimes it works. Stealing from David was never about the money, not really. People steal things for all kinds of reasons. Sometimes it's simply for the reason that they can. For the thrill of it. To see how much they can get away with. That's the part Ali loves.

"I could ruin you or I could kill you."

"You wouldn't though," she says. "You're not that kind of man."

"You don't know what kind of man I am."

"I'm a psychologist, David. I can assure you I do."

He looks over at her and shakes his head. He's disgusted, but Ali knows it's more with himself than her. "Why would you pay your father off? And why would you steal from me to do it?" She shifts toward the window. "You look like you do okay."

"He molested me. And looks can be deceiving."

"That's fucked up."

"You have no idea."

164

"So what? You think you can punish other men for what he did? Is that what this is?"

Ali almost smiles because he's using armchair psychology on her. She catches herself. "I don't know. I just needed him not to go to the press. He's always threatening to leak the story, anonymously, of course."

"Looks like he finally made good on his promise."

"He always does."

"When did it happen?" David closes his eyes. "When did he hurt you?" Ali's soothed by the concern in his voice. She plans to milk it for all it's worth. Even if what she's offering David are partial truths, she appreciates how invested he is in hearing them.

"When I was a teenager. But that's all in the past. I don't like to go there."

"Before the interview with Sarah Shepard," he says, looking directly at her. "Why didn't you just go to the cops?"

Ali laughs. She doesn't mean to, but she does. "You don't know my father."

CHAPTER THIRTY

Ali

Seattle-Tacoma International Airport

A li fastens her seatbelt as the flight attendant belts out the usual spiel. She wasn't expecting to have to hightail it from Seattle to Boston. Not on such short notice. Not with so much on her plate. She has clients scheduled back in Austin and a seminar in San Francisco. Unfortunately, none of that matters because Edward is sick. He has a urinary tract infection, his third one in a very short stint, and he's landed himself in the hospital, leaving her no choice but to fly home to be at his side. After the accident, Edward gave her power of attorney, which means if something occurs that looks serious, she needs to be there. And when someone's a paraplegic, it always seems serious.

As the plane taxis to the runway, Ali thinks back to the first time she and Edward met. It was at a party she almost skipped. It's funny to think now. They almost didn't meet.

That's why thinking about the chance encounter brings her so much joy. She remembers it like it was yesterday. Everyone had been wandering about, tipping back drinks, laughing and chatting amongst themselves. Edward was there with Catherine. Ali was with someone she hadn't been dating long. She couldn't even remember his name.

Later Edward told Ali the story of the first time he laid eyes on her at that party. He loved telling that story. Especially when they were with friends. He'd tell everyone how Deborah had leaned in with a hushed voice and said to him, "Ali is her stage name, although chances are she'll have given you another. Have you met?"

He didn't think so.

"Trust me, you'd remember if you had."

"Yeah, I don't think so."

"Oh, then, you must."

"Who is she?" Edward asked. He had recounted the conversation to Ali later, much later. Ali had smiled and brushed it off, even though she knew everything Deborah had said was true.

"Ali," the woman confessed. "She's the person you want in a room with you when you want to find out if someone is full of shit. You want to know if the person you're dating is wasting your time? Give her ten minutes with them and she'll find out what they really think about their mother, what they were like growing up, if he or she prefers chocolate to vanilla."

"Really." He was intrigued. Not only was Ali strikingly beautiful, she sounded smart and cunning too. Exactly his type.

"You want to know if they're hiding something," Deborah continued.

"If who is hiding something?"

"Catherine. Your date. *Anyone*." She spoke fast, like she had a lot to say and wanted to make sure she got it all out. "I mean, of course they are. Who isn't?"

Edward shrugged. But he didn't respond.

Deborah narrowed her eyes. "Everyone has secrets."

"Do they?"

She placed her hand on his forearm and gave it a squeeze. "Don't be so coy."

"Am I?"

"Private lives are fine, unless someone is being deceptive in a way that will hurt the people she cares about. *That's* Ali. She's very protective. Believe me, you want her in your corner."

"She sounds incredible."

"Yeah, you think so now." The woman nodded. "Just wait until you meet her."

ALI MADE THE FIRST MOVE. SHE INTRODUCED HERSELF AND TALKED about how she knew the host. A former neighbor. She asked how long he'd lived in the area and what he did for a living. *Pediatric oncologist.* It impressed her, but she didn't let on. Edward would tell her later what surprised him most was how easy she was to talk to. A breath of fresh air, he said. This did not surprise her. A conversation connoisseur, Ali had icebreakers for days. She was intentional, careful not to lead with the fact that she has a background in psychology, sex education, literature, and economics. She certainly didn't let on that she's a movie buff, an avid reader, a history nerd, and a bit of a techie. She asked questions instead and let Edward fill in the blanks later.

She asked him about his favorite book, the best meal he'd ever had, where he took his last vacation. Ali listened to his answers, but more than that she made sure to listen to *how* he answered. She noticed what he did with his hands when he spoke, if he chewed at his lip, the way his eyes flickered with emotion, or didn't.

Intimate conversation is Ali's jam. It's an art she knows has little to do with talking dirty or flirtation. She leaned in close so she could hear everything he said. Ali didn't break eye contact. She wanted him to feel like the most important person in the room. And she was sure he did. Edward had her complete and undivided attention. Before he knew it, he told Ali later, just after they'd slept together, he found himself wanting to tell her things he'd never told anyone. Not his best friend. Not his long-time girlfriend, Catherine. Not even his therapist.

Five minutes in, Edward told her his job hadn't felt fulfilling lately. After ten minutes, he mentioned he was nervous about going home for Christmas. After a half hour, he confessed that he'd always been the stable one in his family, that he was tired of being the go-between among his checked-out father and his control-freak mother. He talked about his sister, the fuck-up who'd always been their favorite, despite the fact that she thinks of no one but herself.

The drink in his hand went mostly unconsumed. She wanted to make him feel like it was just the two of them in the room, like the rest of the party had drifted away, and it worked. When their eyes met, what she saw reflected back was a sense of familiarity. That feeling enveloped her like a warm summer breeze. She was tuned in, tapped in, turned on. She smiled. This is what she came for.

He must have sensed he'd said too much, so he suddenly straightened his back and shook his head. He downed his drink; and told Ali that suddenly his throat felt tight. The room had to be ten degrees warmer. "Damn," he said. "Look at me, dumping my entire life story on you." He shook his head. "I'm sorry. I'm sure you didn't come to Sharon and Dave's engagement party to listen to a boring physician talk about his childhood wounds."

"It's Deborah."

"I'm sorry?"

"It's *Deborah* and Dave's party."

"Gosh, that's right." He shook his head. "I don't know why I said Sharon." *What was wrong with him?*

"Don't be sorry," she said kindly. "It's been a pleasure getting to know you."

He studied her curiously. "Are you sure you aren't a therapist?"

She laughed, but she didn't give a direct answer. Instead, she told him she loves talking to people. And not long after, she looked away, and the ambient music and background chatter slowly rose, reminding him that there were other people in the room.

Edward smiled. It was sweet, that moment. After they broke apart to rejoin their dates and the rest of the party, he looked at her from across the room a little nervously. *What the hell just happened? What had gotten into him, pouring his heart out to a total stranger?*

He couldn't know this, not then. But the exact moment when someone stopped being average and became an actual person, with a dark and complex story beyond his or her 150-character Instalook bio, *that's* when Ali came alive.

They didn't speak again for the rest of the night. But later, as everyone said their goodbyes to the hosts, they met again in the logjam at the door. She let the awkwardness hang in the air for a second longer than necessary and then smiled at him in a friendly way to let him know there was no harm, no foul. He looked relieved. She wasn't creeped out or going to cause any trouble.

He told her it was nice to meet her, and the two of them laughed awkwardly, although her eyes conveyed something different, something shared. Intimacy. "I hope Christmas goes okay," she said. "Family stuff can be treacherous." Then he walked out the door and got in his car. He thought he'd never see her again.

He told her later that he'd thought of her on the drive home, with a slight unease, the kind that made him question his entire life. He didn't need to worry. Ali wouldn't share the things he told her, not with anyone. Because honestly? No one would care. It's not like he confessed to having several hacked-up bodies in a freezer in his basement or to running million-dollar scams on the elderly. Ali's seen a lot. She knows most confessions are rarely as unique as people think they are. But Edward didn't know that. He just knew he had an out-of-character, personal encounter with a beautiful woman who had kind eyes and a friendly smile. He shared things that were deeply personal. Then it was over. She left and took his secrets with her.

Until he ran into her again, the following summer at another party. He bumped into her by the cooler. They chatted briefly about the weather. Ali has an excellent memory. Her breath quickened as she asked how Christmas went with his family. He didn't know it at the time, but this is what she came for. She doesn't have a photographic memory, but she can recall details about people that go back decades. Even her archives have archives. Edward looked at her, brows raised. "Jesus, that's right, I told you that." His face reddened, but not from the dead heat of summer. He'd forgotten her name, and it was obvious.

She stuck out her hand and smiled. "It's okay," she said. "We met forever ago. At Deborah and Dave's engagement party."

"I remember."

"I'm Ali," she said. "Ali Brown."

CHAPTER THIRTY-ONE

Ethan

I finally got a break in the Lucas Bennett case. Max called and said they got a lead from the police tip hotline. He told me the initial tip led the caller to him as the lead detective on the case. The caller, a neighbor at the apartment building where the senator's son lived, told Max that he distinctly recalled seeing two people, a male and a female, either enter or exit, Lucas Bennett's apartment around the time of his death. The male was a plumber, and the woman was dressed in a fancy trench coat. The caller also did not believe that Lucas Bennett killed himself. Ethan wasn't sure why the caller thought his opinion mattered that much.

Thankfully, when Max calls to relay the information, I am not in the school drop-off line. "I thought you might want the address so you could speak to him. Thought it might help with your case. Hypothetically speaking."

"Of course. I'd love to," I say, grabbing something to write with.

"Just don't mention the PD or how you got the information. Act like a curious neighbor or the press or something, I don't know."

"The press, that's a good one."

"You'll figure it out, I'm sure."

"I appreciate this, Max. You have no idea."

"I do. Have some idea. Anyway," he sighs. "The senator wants his son's death put to bed. He doesn't need any bad press, not with elections coming up. Sympathy is fine. Skeletons coming out of the closet are not."

"Got it. No problem. You're doing me a solid. I won't mess it up." I owe Max plenty of favors, but we both know this isn't really that. He's throwing me a bone. He's aware of the financial incentive on my end. Unlike Max, I'm on my own payroll. He'll always have more cases than he has time to solve. And a pension at that.

Of course, what Max doesn't know is that I am personally involved with a suspect in the case. Or that I have a stake that's more than merely financial. He doesn't know that I'm sleeping with a woman who is potentially tied to Lucas Bennett, or that the woman in the trench coat matches Ali's description to a T.

All things considered, especially the last one, how could I possibly tell Max no?

THE NEIGHBOR, ALFRED FAVERO III, AN OLD MAN EASILY PUSHING eighty, has a memory like an elephant. I tell him this after he describes seeing a woman that looks exactly like Ali. He recalls the exact date and time of her coming and going.

"You just wait until you have nothing to do but watch the comings and goings of your neighbors. It isn't the blessing you think it is," he says.

This man doesn't know that this is already the case and I'm

half his age, but I want him to feel special. I'll get more information that way.

His hands shake as he speaks. "Lloyd's Plumbing Co.," he tells me. "That was the name of the company I read on the front of the man's shirt." He points to the apartment across the hall. "He came from that apartment. Bennett's apartment."

"And the woman? Had you seen her before?"

"I can't recall seeing her, no. But it was late when I saw her, and usually I go to bed by 10:30. Just shortly after the ten o'clock news. That night, however, I'd had terrible indigestion brought on by Mildred's lasagna. It kept me up." He looks down the hall, one way and then the other. "Mildred's my sister."

"She sounds lovely."

"You'd have to know her." He leans on his cane and shifts his footing. "Sometimes I have insomnia. But that night it had been for sure Mildred's lasagna. I always eat it, and I always call her to tell her how much I enjoyed it, even though it's a lie. Just a little white one, though. She gets mad if I don't. And trust me, you don't want to see Millie mad."

"Women," I say, with an eye roll.

"I feel bad, but I know how much effort it takes to recreate the dish mother was famous for, Millie makes sure to tell me every time. So, I eat it. Even if it nearly kills me each time."

Mr. Favero III describes hearing a knock across the hall on Lucas Bennett's door around one a.m. the morning before Lucas's body was discovered. Alfred tells me he was worried because sometimes the kid liked to have parties that kept him up and he was concerned this would be one of those nights.

"I'd been meaning to have a talk with him," Alfred sighs. "I just never saw him in the daytime. He tended to come and go at night."

"And the plumber? You didn't see anyone else? Any friends of Lucas's? People that regularly came by?"

"The plumber I saw come and go several times. The woman, she knocked on the door in the early morning hours. Like I said, maybe around one or so. When Lucas opened the door, she called out, 'Surprise!'"

"And then what happened?"

"Then she opened the coat, and let it fall until it was just hanging there, off her shoulders. It finally stopped down around her elbows. She was naked underneath!"

My eyes narrow. "You saw all this through the peephole?"

"Sure did. Despite the indigestion, it turned out to be the best night I've had in a long time. I promised myself I'd make a point of staying up late more often."

I SIT AT MY DESK THINKING OF LUCAS BENNETT'S NEIGHBOR AND what he told me. Based on his description, the woman sure sounds like Ali.

But I've run a lot of investigations, and I know how eyewitness testimony can be. I shuffle through the case file and then look at the neighbor's statement. I've seen this scenario dozens of times. I just have to give it some thought. It's been a while.

Before our home was invaded and Abby was killed, I worked for the FBI. I'd had many roles over the years, but at that time I was working for the FBI's National Center for the Analysis of Violent Crime (NCAVC) as a criminal investigative analyst, also known as a criminal profiler. My job was to compile and compare data from similar crimes and offenders to create a profile of a suspect. The basic premise is that behavior reflects personality. For example, in a homicide case, it was my job as an FBI agent to glean insight into personality through questions about the murderer's behavior at four crime phases. First, I'd consider what fantasy or plan, or both, the murderer might have had in place before the act. What triggered the murderer to act some days and not others?

Then I'd look at the method and manner: What type of victim

or victims did the murderer select? What was the method and manner of murder: shooting, stabbing, strangulation, or something else? Also, how was the body disposed of? Did the murder and body disposal take place all at one scene, or multiple scenes? And after the crime, was there any specific post-offense behavior? Had the murderer tried to inject him or herself into the investigation by reacting to media reports or contacting investigators?

In the Roberts/Bennett cases, I can easily answer questions two and three. The first, I'm still working out. But it's the last question that gets me. If Ali is responsible for killing these men, what does she know of my involvement in the case?

CHAPTER THIRTY-TWO

I hate old people. They're crusty and wrinkled and gross. And worse, they make a habit of sticking their noses where they don't belong. I don't know why they think they're special, as though incontinence and losing their hearing are something to aspire to. They demand respect because they've been through world wars. They were here before the television or the internet existed, but who cares? We all die someday and all they're doing is just sitting around waiting. I mean, what's the point? They're taking up resources that the young and the useful members of society need. They're a drain on society with their social security and all the medicine they need, just so their bodies can function the way they once did, the way they're supposed to.

Typically, I don't let such things bother me too much. I'm only reminded when I have to be around them and get a whiff of mothballs and old cheese, which thankfully isn't too often. Unfortunately, there was the Italian. He had that look about him, the kind that said I exist solely to cause you trouble. And that's exactly what he did.

He wasn't surprised to see me return to the building. He looked a little excited. Like it was the best thing that had happened to him all week, and it probably was. He couldn't wait to tell me about the "murder next door."

Not only did he dish out details I already knew, he did so over a Pyrex filled with lasagna. It was warm and covered in a dish towel. I meant to only have a bite, but I ended up eating half the dish. He invited me into his apartment because old people are gullible and lonely.

You should have seen his face as he went on and on about how the cops thought it was a suicide, but he knew better because he knew the kid, and he was the kind who might have an enemy or two. The way he said it, you'd have thought they were best friends. You would have thought we were two sleuths on a mission to solve a wicked crime together. The kind of thing, like an old war story, that would bind us together for life, even if the rest of his was significantly shorter. "It's such a shame he was so young," I said.

"He had his entire life ahead of him."

For someone who thought the kid was a nuisance, he sure had a lot of nostalgia and sadness balled up inside. Good news is, now they can be together in heaven.

It was easy to lure him to the stairwell. He didn't want me to leave. I asked him to show me out. He said he preferred taking the stairs. It kept him young. "Elevators are for old people," he told me with a wink.

"They're for lazy people," I said with a smile, right before I gave him a good, hard shove. It's a real shame, old people being as feeble and clumsy as they are. May he rest in peace.

CHAPTER THIRTY-THREE

Ali

Boston

Time is a thief. When Ali flew from Seattle to Boston she was not expecting to spend three days on a tiny cot in the hospital, but that's exactly what she ends up doing. It takes an immense amount of time to pretend you love someone, and if this doesn't make it look real, she doesn't know what does. Edward's UTI came on quick, just like the others. This one, like the last, led to sepsis.

When Ali first arrived, the doctors didn't expect Edward to pull through. Ali didn't, either. But he did.

He always does.

It's not that she wishes Edward would die. It's just, well, how else is she supposed to get out of this?

Their relationship was never meant to be a long-term thing. Although, sitting at his bedside in the hospital, she can see that's how it's turned out and that's how it's looking for the foreseeable future.

She never would have married him. Not for real. It wasn't her fault her new fiancé ended up in a wheelchair. It wasn't his fault either. He had been participating in one of his triathlons for charity. The kind of activity she pretended to find endearing, but actually thought was quite annoying. Anyone who's training for a triathlon, well, you can bet your bottom dollar, that's *all* they talk about. Ali heard about it for weeks on end. The runs and the swims, the saddle soreness from the bike. He never shut up. She was so ready for the event to be over, she literally counted down the days for him, marking them off on the calendar in his kitchen with red ink. On the days she was away on business, Edward kept it up. In hindsight, they were counting down *not* to something celebratory, but to a date when neither of their lives would ever be the same.

An elderly man, blinded by the sun, had slammed his car through the race barriers, barreling into Edward as he was on his final turn. The car dragged him twenty-six feet. It was terrible luck, one of those wrong place, wrong time situations. For both Edward and Ali. She hadn't planned on being his wife, and she certainly never planned on being his caretaker. But there was an awful lot of money at stake. And Ali isn't one to turn down a buck. So, now, here she is doing both. Here she is sitting vigil at his bedside. Here she is waiting for him to die.

Being a widow sounds refreshing. She wrote that in her journal, just now. It's something she thinks every day. To have her freedom back is her greatest wish. She can't wait. Not only will she have a new title, widow instead of *wife*, she'll never have to work another day in her life. Not unless she wants to and she won't have to run her petty scams anymore. Unless she wants to keep doing that too. And she probably will. How boring would life be without the hustle?

The doctors say it's possible Edward will walk again one day. Only time and a lot of hard work will tell. He's gaining strength every day, and he tries his hardest to make things easy for her. Unless, of course, work calls her away. Then it's a different story.

⸻

ONCE ALI HAS GOTTEN EDWARD SETTLED AT HOME, SHE PLOTS HER escape. Then the worst part, she tells him about it. He's been sulking all day.

Now, it's dinnertime and he's refusing to eat. "Do you really have to go?"

"You're doing so much better," Ali says, brushing his bangs away from his eyes. "Look at you."

"I know, but I miss you when you're gone. It's tough being here all alone, and every time you leave, I seem to end up in the hospital."

"I think it's a ploy to get me back here."

"Maybe it's a ploy to make you stay."

"Oh, Edward." She knows he's joking, at least partly. "Your mom's coming. And she's a far better cook."

"But I want my wife."

Ali hates that word. She nearly flinches. She's acclimated to it over time. Hiding non-verbal cues takes practice. "I know."

"You took vows, Ali." His eyes darken and Ali hates when he gets this way. She wonders, along with his antibiotic if she'd given him his antidepressant. With everything going on, it's possible she forgot. He's perfectly capable of handling his own medication, but when Ali's home he insists she wait on him. "You promised, remember? In sickness and in health."

Ali contemplates placing the pillow over his head and bearing down with all her might. She had once researched the number of ways to kill a person and not get caught. In the old days, women used to use hatpins to puncture holes in the backs of their husband's throats while they slept. Ali thought about it. She wondered how she'd get Edward to keep his mouth open long enough. She wonders if anyone ever journaled about *that*. This is the problem. Where do you find this information? The library? The internet? Where? Success usually leaves clues, but not this kind of success. Also, Edward has very sharp teeth. What a nightmare it would be if he woke up in the middle of it. It's kind of difficult to explain away losing your hand that way.

Insulin under the tongue could take care of the problem. But she doesn't have any of that handy. At least not at the moment, and if there were an autopsy, it would probably show up. Better to wait for natural causes, Ali ultimately decided. Although, who is she kidding? Edward has proven he has at least nine lives.

"I did promise," she replies softly. "That was the best day of my life. And I'm here, aren't I? I've always come when you've needed me. And I always will."

Edward looks away, toward the television, which is muted. "I saw your interview with Sarah Shepard."

"Yeah?"

He glares at the TV, refusing to look at her. He gets like this when she leaves. Unpredictable and despondent. "I heard she's missing."

"Missing?"

"Yeah," he says harshly. "As in they can't find her, *missing*. As in vanished, *missing*."

"Sarah Shepard? That's—"

"It's all over the news, Ali."

"I don't watch the news," she tells him, although it isn't entirely true. Three days tossing and turning on a makeshift bed in a hospital and you start doing a lot of things you don't normally do.

"Bad things happen when you go away. That interview was disastrous for your career."

"It could have been." She sighs. "But it wasn't. My career is fine."

"You don't need to travel anymore. An office here in Boston—that's all you need. Make people come to you. Or don't. It's not like we need the money."

Ali surveys the condo. She contemplates staying. But she knows she can't. This place has never felt like home to her. Less so after everything had to be rearranged to accommodate Edward's wheelchair. He has therapy equipment crammed into practically every crevice. Their marital bed was replaced with a hospital bed. It wasn't supposed to be permanent. None of this was. Now Ali lays with him until he falls asleep and then she gets up and goes to the futon in the corner. She sleeps like a baby and dreams of ways to end this.

"What's gotten into you?" she whispers as she rests her head on his shoulder. They're sitting on the couch staring out at the skyline. "I'll only be gone a few days."

He pinches her arm, hard.

Ali pulls away. "Ouch."

She hates it when he does this. Sometimes he can't find the words, and he wants to show her how it feels. He wants her to know how frustrating it is to lose control of your life. What he can't understand is that she does. Not in the same way, but who said pain was equal?

She stands and then bends down and kisses his forehead. To prove a point, she walks away and glances over her shoulder and says, "You never had a problem with me traveling before."

"That was then." He throws the remote at the wall, breaking it into several pieces. At least this time it wasn't the TV. Ali stares at him until finally he meets her eye. He sucks his lip between his teeth. "Things are different now. Remember the accident?" He motions toward his chair.

Ali shakes her head. "How could I forget?"

CHAPTER THIRTY-FOUR

Ethan

I promise myself I'm going to cut things off with Ali. Nadia makes me swear. She also threatens to tell Max. Then I didn't end it right away and Nadia made good on her threat. When Max catches wind of my situation, he makes me swear on our friendship and our professional relationship, no more contact, lest I continue to put the investigation, his job, and my life, in jeopardy.

Ali spends three days messaging me almost nonstop. She's out of town and I figure what's the harm in a little harmless conversation? After all, she's hundreds of miles away.

Ali had previously told me she was headed to Boston for work. I relayed the info to Nadia who reached out to a friend that lives near Cambridge. She asked her to follow Ali from the airport.

One morning Nadia comes in late, holding two cups of coffee set in a takeout tray in one hand and a large envelope in the other. "Sorry, I'm late," she says. "I had to stop by the print shop."

She slams the envelope down on my desk and then takes her

coffee from the tray and places mine on my desk. I reach in and pull out several photographs. "You're never gonna believe it."

I lay the photos out on my desk, arranging them like puzzle pieces. I lean forward to study them closely. My stomach tightens and my mouth goes dry as I go through them one by one. The sight of Ali makes me slightly dizzy.

There's a shot of her entering Mass General Hospital in Boston. There are shots of her standing outside the hospital near the emergency entrance presumably getting air and messaging me. There are pictures of her staring at her phone, photos of her sitting in a car in the parking garage. I think of her there messaging me, writing amusing texts, flirty texts, dirty texts.

In another photo, she wheels a man from the hospital entrance and helps transfer him from a wheelchair to an SUV that's waiting at the curb.

In the next set of photos, the SUV has pulled up in front of a high-rise building. Then Nadia pulls up a video on her phone and plays it for me. I watch as Ali unloads the chair from the back of the SUV and readies it for its occupant. She's pushing it to the passenger side door, and she's helping him into it. She works the chair like a pro, setting it up just right, applying the brake, holding it so it doesn't move, loading several bags of belongings on the man's lap, flinging an overnight bag over her shoulder. I can tell this isn't her first rodeo.

The last set of photos shows Ali greeting the doorman with a tight smile, chatting with him. The final photo shows her disappearing into the building, wheeling the man through the doors.

According to the timestamps, she was messaging me about having full days, working with clients. In the past twenty-four hours, she's only written sporadically, rarely initiating conversation, but she always replies.

"Is it family?" I ask Nadia, lifting my coffee from the Styrofoam tray. "It has to be family." I point to the photograph of her positioning the wheelchair at the passenger side of the SUV. "Because *that* does not look like a cold-blooded killer."

"Have you ever heard of Ted Bundy? Or Perry Smith?"

"Sure."

"How about Colonel Russell Williams?"

"Let me guess, also fond of murder?"

"Yeah, *and* he was a pilot. Supposedly, he flew the British royal family around the world. I read he had a penchant for dressing up in women's lingerie. Talk about a double life."

"You sure seem to know a lot about serial killers."

Nadia smiles. "It's a fetish."

"I don't want to know."

She grins from ear to ear. She stabs her pointy finger at one photograph, pinning it to the desk. "That guy there is her husband."

I'm not shocked. At least I don't mean to be. For as long as I've been in this line of work, I've seen a lot. I don't know how I could have missed this. Except that I never checked. "Did you find out anything about her parents? Mother? Father?"

"This isn't enough?"

"I don't think she's our killer."

"Why? Because she helped a dude into a wheelchair? A man that she happens to be *married* to."

"No, because I haven't found a motive."

"What motive did Gacy or Williams or Bundy have other than they were fucking crazy?"

Nadia has a point.

"She screws anything with legs. What else do you need, boss?"

"That's not funny."

"You said you weren't going to see her anymore."

"I'm not."

"I don't believe you. I'm going to talk to Max again."

"What for?"

"He needs to put more resources on this. I'm out of favors and I don't have many friends as it is."

"You and me?" I motion between the two of us. "We don't have any say in a police investigation. Or have you forgotten? We're in private practice with paying civilian clients. Leave Max out of it. He's done enough."

"I should know. I'm the one sleeping with him."

"Please don't tell me anymore."

"He'll do what I say."

"Great," I tell her, leaving it at that. I don't want to discuss my friend or the mistake he is making. Max is a married man who should not be sleeping with my assistant. Not only is she half his age, I sometimes doubt her sanity. But then, who am I to talk? To say anything would be the pot calling the kettle black. At least I'm not married. There's one thing going for me.

"Ali," I say to Nadia. "Has she been on dates in Boston? Through the app? I mean—has she been seeing anyone?"

"I don't know for sure." Nadia takes a long sip from her cup. "I don't think so. From what my friend tells me, she's mostly been at the hospital with her *husband*. Probably not much time for dating."

Her emphasis on the word husband annoys me. Nadia's driving her point home. But I've known a lot of women like Ali Brown, and if there's one thing they have in common, it's that they never stay committed for long. Single, either, for that matter.

"He's a quadriplegic," I say.

"What?"

"A quad—"

"No," she says, shaking her head. "He's a paraplegic." She points to a photo. "See here, he has use of his arms."

"Paraplegic—whatever. My point is, you can understand how she might want to—you know—date other people. And there's a saying. You can't turn a sports car into a minivan."

"You're a terrible person."

"Am I?"

Nadia rolls her eyes. "Jesus, boss. You really need to get a grip."

"Stop calling me that. And I have a grip."

"You act like you're in love with her."

"Love is a bit of a stretch."

"Well, you're acting like a teenager."

I smile. "I feel like one."

WHEN I RETURN FROM LUNCH, NADIA'S MOOD HAS LIFTED, AND she's all smiles.

"What now?" I ask, flipping through the stack of mail on her desk.

She nods. "Guess who's back?"

I take two envelopes and leave the rest. "Ali?"

She lets out a long sigh. When I look up, her nostrils are flaring. "No, your *favorite*—and by that I mean your *only*—client."

"Shit." I glance toward my office. "Camille."

"Bingo."

"She doesn't have an appointment."

Nadia comes around the desk, takes the remote from the coffee table in the waiting area, and flips on the TV. "She never has an appointment."

"You're in my chair again," I say to Camille as I close my office door.

"And here I took you for a gentleman."

"What can I do for you? I have a meeting in five minutes."

"I'm hoping you have something for me. I'm hoping I didn't come all the way down here only to find out I'm wasting my time *and* my money?"

"I'd hate to disappoint you—"

"I'd hate that, too." She stands and walks from behind my desk, standing close to me. Too close. She leans in, leveling with me. "If you don't tell me you've made at least some progress on finding my father's killer, then I'm afraid this is going to be a farewell trip. You're not the only investigator in town, Mr. Lane."

"No, I'm not." I don't take kindly to threats. "But I'm probably the only one you can afford. And certainly the only one who's going to put up with the fact that you're a giant pain in the ass."

"Speaking of—" she says, brow arched. "I know that before me, before I brought you this case, that you were about to have to close up shop. I've known that all along. You see, I didn't actually mind that you're barely keeping your shit together." She takes two steps back and places her hands on her hips. "Why? Because it gives a person that edge, it gives you a certain hunger that most people simply don't have. But now—" She swipes her hand in the air. "Well, now, I'm questioning whether I've misjudged you."

I glance out at the waiting area. My appointment is early. A potential client, a client I must land if I'm going to make rent next month, is standing there talking to Nadia. Not only do I need the business, I need time to finish this case. The last thing I need is Camille causing a scene. But I wouldn't put it past her, not for a minute. Camille Roberts is the type of woman who, if she goes down, is going to make damn sure you go down with her.

"Listen," I say, attempting to defuse the situation. I just need to get her out of my office, and from there out of the building.

Her gaze lowers to the floor. "I'm going to have to start selling off his things."

I don't respond because I'm staring at the TV. Ali's face flashes across the screen, and then there's a spilt screen, with Ali and Sarah Shepard, before it cuts to a clip of the interview.

"His paintings will have to go. And at least two of his horses. God, do you know how humiliating this is?" Her hands fly in the air. "His horses!"

"It's okay," I say in a way that reflects my attention is elsewhere.

"I bet you have no idea the upkeep on a horse."

"What?"

"Are you even listening?" Camille raises her voice so that I'm forced to look at her. The woman in my waiting area is staring, and I curse Bethany for her nonsensical idea of using glass as a barrier between my office and the rest of the place. Finally, Camille takes the hint and follows my gaze. "Oh God, not her again!"

At first, I'm taken aback because I think she's referring to the woman in my waiting room. Then I realize she's looking at the television.

Camille goes quiet for exactly the amount of time it takes her to read the ticker scrolling across the screen, and not a second later. "They found her body," she gasps. "My God. This is horrible." Her hands fly to her mouth. "I loved Sarah Shepard."

This does not surprise me. But what Camille Roberts says next certainly does.

She shakes her head slowly. "It makes sense that Ali was her final interview."

"Why?"

Camille looks at me like I'm an idiot for asking the question. "That girl brings trouble wherever she goes."

I check the time. "Huh."

"It's like a curse."

"How do you know?"

"I grew up with her."

"What do you mean you grew up with her?"

"Are you even listening?" Her eyes narrow as she places her hands on her hips. "Are you dense?"

She's speaking as though I'm a mind reader. She's not making any sense. No woman wants to hear that, so rather than argue I simply say, "I've been accused a time or two."

"Ali Brown is my stepsister."

CHAPTER THIRTY-FIVE

Ethan

I suspect Ali killed Donovan Roberts. And I think I understand why. I invite Ali for dinner, not sure what to expect. I am going to confront her over the fact that I believe she killed her stepfather. What I don't understand is why she killed the other men, and I want to know. I really, really do.

The scene is set. The food has been ordered and delivered. Italian. I take great care in setting everything out, using plates and dishes that make it appear that I cooked it myself. I place candles on the table because I know Ali appreciates that kind of thing.

I spent all day tidying the house and mowing the lawn. The last thing left to do is shower and throw on something decent. I'll admit, while my goal is to corner her into a confession, I wouldn't turn down sex should it come to that. And judging by the lewd text messages she sent this afternoon, I have a feeling it might.

After I've showered and shaved, I light the candles, only to realize I've forgotten the wine. I'd meant to pick some up on the way home, but I was distracted by Ali's nude selfies. Since I wasn't planning on drinking, wine wasn't at the forefront of my mind. Payday was.

I like Ali.

But I like my career more.

It's nice to have electricity.

Feeding your children and health insurance aren't bad either.

I now realize that the wine is imperative. We all know what happens when inhibitions are lowered, and when Ali mentioned having a rough week, I told her I'd have some ready and waiting. I want her to pour her little heart out. So I leave a note on the door and dash out, hitting up the corner store. Admittedly, they don't have the best selection, but something is better than nothing, and it's not like I'll be drinking it anyway.

When I get home, Ali is sitting on my front porch. "You changed the locks."

I smile. She's wearing a short skirt and thin top that hangs off her bare shoulder. She stands and smooths her skirt. "It's good to see you too."

I invite her inside. My demeanor is a little cold on purpose. I want her to work for my affection and I have a feeling that if I play my cards right, she will.

We move toward the kitchen where I unwrap the bottle of wine, fish around for the bottle opener in a drawer, and then use it to remove the cork. I pour two glasses and hand her one. Then I raise mine. "A toast," I say.

She eyes me suspiciously. Ali is not stupid. "What are we toasting to?"

"Your marriage."

Her face loses a little color, but she recovers quickly. "To my marriage." She touches her glass to mine and takes a long gulp.

"You're full of surprises, aren't you?"

"Yes. But I never said I wasn't married."

"You never said you were."

"You didn't ask."

I corner her against the wall. "Where's the gun?"

"Easy, Rambo." She pushes against my chest. "I came straight from the airport. It's at home."

I pat her down. She enjoys it a little more than I'd like. "Show me your purse."

"It's in the car."

I think back to her sitting on my porch. She's right. She wasn't holding anything. "It makes me wet when you get all worked up." She leans forward and kisses me on the mouth. I taste the wine on her lips.

"I know who you are," I say, but it's too late. She's already fumbling with my belt and then the button on my jeans. The zipper I help her with.

She takes me in her hand and works her magic. When she sees I am dissolving with pleasure, she stops, and looks at me in a way that suggests she's considering that if she deprives me now, I might cave or beg, or make a gesture toward something more. At first I do nothing, letting the uncertainty hang in the air.

Ali lifts her shirt, pulls it over her head, and drops it at my feet. She pushes her skirt up above her hips and takes my hand, placing it between her legs. She moves my fingers mechanically. I offer little in the way of help. "You think you know me," she says. "But you don't."

She's taunting me and it's working. My finger dips beneath her panties, searching. I am tormented with desire. But I refuse to give in to her. Ali grows desperate. She pushes my hand forward, before dropping to her knees. She takes me into her mouth, and her hands work double-time. She moves swiftly up and down my shaft and then stops, slows, and starts again. Her mouth absorbs me fully. I take a fistful of her hair and tug. Then I push her forward, easing her into it, then move faster, controlling the pace. She looks up at me doe-eyed, in a way that we both know is an act. She's good, and I come with such violent delight that I think we're both a little surprised. Then I lean over with gratitude and tenderness, and murmur, "You're perfect on paper, but you lie to my face."

"What a lovely observation," she says, wiping her mouth with the corner of her hand. "What now?"

"Now, we eat."

I extend my hand and help her to her feet. "Good. I'm starving."

She follows me to the table, grabbing her wineglass on the way. "You won't believe the week I've had."

I pull her chair out and motion for her to take a seat. "Sounds like we have a lot to discuss."

I take a bit of Italian meatballs from the dish and scoop them onto my plate. "So, tell me about Donovan Roberts."

"My stepfather?" She stabs at her plate of pasta and looks me straight in the eye. "He's dead."

"I know. And you killed him?"

"You ask like it's a question. But you're the investigator. You tell me."

"And the others?"

She cocks her head. "What?"

"I know you have a knack for making sure the men in your life end up dead. What I want to know is why."

She laughs. A little at first, but then it becomes hysterical. "So that's what you think of me?" she asks between fits.

"You haven't answered my question."

"You know what?" She throws her napkin at me. Her aim is quite impressive. It hits me in the head. "Fuck you, Ethan."

Her eyes convey fury, and maybe a little hurt. I think she's going to kill me.

IT STARTS OUT SLOW. THE SLIGHTEST TWINGE, COUPLED WITH AN inkling that something isn't right. It quickly becomes more than that. Embarrassed, I excuse myself from the table and retreat to the bedroom, which I soon realize is a smart move.

I haven't even fully closed the door before the twinges stop and the pain takes over, engulfing me. Internal heat rages throughout my rib cage, descending downward, spiraling into my abdominal cavity. It effortlessly pulls me under until I fold in two. Thirty seconds ago, I was completely fine. Better than fine. It was the happiest moment of my life. I was about to finally solve the Roberts case. I was about to finally be right in a conversation with a woman. That in and of itself is a real feat.

Now I'm dying.

Clutching my midsection in complete agony, I lean forward, pressing my body against the door, slamming it shut. I flip the lock as a cold sweat sweeps over me. Within seconds, my lungs seize. No matter how much air I attempt to suck in, it isn't enough. My vision blurs as my breath comes out in spurts. I pant like a dog on a hot day.

The room takes on a very distinct smell, reminding me of burnt flesh. It steeps the air in the combination of a liver-like scent and sulfur. While the fire may be internal, the smell isn't. My stomach knots, clenches, twists, and turns. The pain is relentless as it radiates outward, its tendrils wrapping around every inch of me. It feels like I'm being skinned alive, only from the inside out. With every inhale, the sensation tightens its grip, until I can no longer think straight.

Until I can no longer see a way out of this.

Until misery is all there is.

Whispering jumbled prayers, I pray to God, to Moses, to Buddha—I pray to anyone who will listen. I just need them to make this stop.

They don't. And it doesn't.

The searing heat engulfing my insides only intensifies. I grit my teeth so hard I fear they may chip off in my mouth. Shock forces me deep inside myself, making it hard to know what is real and what isn't. It feels like someone is prying my mouth open, holding my jaw in place, pouring battery acid down my throat. It feels like a Molotov cocktail has been buried deep within my belly. A ticking time bomb planted and detonated.

But no. It's just me in this room, alone with my poor decisions.

My mind tries to rationalize. This cannot be happening.

But it is very much happening.

As I writhe from side to side, I force myself to focus.

My eyes scan the bedroom. What can possibly save me now? My phone? *I left it in the kitchen.* Paramedics? *There isn't enough time.*

Water. What I need is water. Something, *anything,* to soothe the burning. I drag myself up, bracing my palms against my thighs. If only I hadn't been so stupid. If only I could get a handle on this.

Two steps are all it takes for me to realize what a pipe dream that is. Time slows to nothing. Internally, layers of flesh are being serrated and filleted. Slices of organs are being peeled away; shallow layers of my innards are slowly separating. Then, with a fiery explosion, what remains disintegrates into nothing. It's all happening in slow motion and I can feel everything.

A pulsating sound pings between my ears. It starts out high-pitched and shrill, and then it dims, but it plays on repeat, so I know what's coming. A cacophony of nails on a chalkboard.

If death has a sound, this is it.

I give up trying to focus on anything else. It's pointless.

My legs buckle, and my body falls to the floor with a heavy thud. The rest of me is somewhere else, halfway to hell.

This is not how this night was supposed to go.

Slinking forward, serpent-like, I inch toward the bathroom. I get nowhere fast, so I shift direction, making it to the bed, where I force myself upward. The room spins like a Tilt-A-Whirl as I sway precariously from side to side. It reminds me of my firstborn learning to walk. It reminds me of carnival trips with my children, memories that will be forgotten instead of made.

Knowing sentimentality can only get me so far, I hobble onward, still holding onto the hope that I survive to see my children's faces once again. Hoping I'll get another chance to hear them laugh. Although I know I probably won't. Right now, there is only one goal: to find water.

It won't save me. But it might buy me some time.

The bathroom is the wrong call, I realize, as I grip the inside of the doorframe. I dig my fingernails into the wood, thinking I should have gone through with the remodel. What an unforgiving place to die.

I hadn't thought the misery could get worse.

I was wrong.

The contractions deep in my gut continue to sweep over me, crashing like tall waves, each one worse than the one before. Eventually, I lose my handle on the doorframe and with it, my footing. I fall forward, endlessly forward, until my skull hits the edge of the sink and a hard crack ensues.

I'd hoped it would end there, but it doesn't. Instead, I am witness to my suffering, as everything slows. This could just as easily be happening to someone else, and if it weren't for the relentless tearing in my stomach, maybe I could pretend that it was.

The blood though, I can't ignore. It trickles out of the corner of my mouth, vibrant against the white marble floor. Brick red and sweet, it coats my lips. I inhale the metallic scent; the warmth brings me comfort. Everything is so cold.

My mouth fills and as I spit blood onto the floor, I see that in the fall, I've bitten off a sliver of my tongue. It looks out of place lying there all pink and moist, covered in tiny bumps. My fingers reach out to touch it. It feels muscular and rough, like something I might have once fished out of the ocean. I cup it in the palm of my hand. For what reason, I don't know. To save it? Just in case? What a silly thought. A last vestige of hope.

My cheek pressed against the cold tile. I think, *so this is where it ends*. There's a rattling in my chest, the kind you hear stories about.

It tells me I don't have long.

Still, my stomach and chest continue to heave, and my body clings desperately to life, a reminder that it refuses to give up long after the mind has. Clawing my way along the smooth marble, I move toward the toilet, but once there, I am too tired to even lift my head.

I allow my eyes to close, and I say a silent prayer that whatever comes next, comes quick. I pray that my children never see me like this, that they never know how I suffered in the end. Then, I wait for the bright white light, but what I get instead is a knock at the bedroom door. It's soft at first and then more urgent. I hear a muffled voice, so familiar, followed by desperate pounding.

It doesn't matter. I can't open the door, even if I wanted to. I have no idea what killed me, but I sure as hell know who did.

CHAPTER THIRTY-SIX

Ethan

When the bathroom door opens, I am not expecting to see men's shoes in my face. I'm expecting to see Ali, or hopefully, paramedics. But no, the doctor has come. At least that's how he identifies himself. At first, I don't believe him, even though you can be anything you want these days.

"Dr. Kemp here," he says with an even tone. "I've come to help."

I blink rapidly several times. At this point I've been in and out of consciousness several times and a part of my tongue is gripped inside the palm of my hand. Anything is possible. "It's possible," I say, with a wince. "I'm dead and this is hell."

"You're not dead," he tells me, making a clucking sound with his mouth. "What a terrible, terrible shame."

He leans down and gets right in my face, so close that I can smell his breath. It's minty. Not at all like I expected, and a welcome respite from the scent of my own. The closer he gets, the more he comes into focus and I realize I know him.

It's the man from Nadia's photos. Only he's not in a wheel-chair. He's standing, and he's placing his fancy shoe on my neck, cutting off my air supply. Things get really strange the closer you are to death. It's like a dream where your mind puts the most random memories together, unfamiliar faces on familiar people, friends from the past, become people in the future. His face is the same.

He lets off my neck. He's distracted, it seems. I suck in several deep breaths, and the more oxygen I inhale, the more my eyes can focus. I reach up and grip his pant leg, hoisting myself up. *Lloyd's Plumbing*, his shirt reads. He has a knife in his right hand. Not a typical tool of the trade, but by this point I've figured out that he hasn't come to fix the toilet.

"She's so much trouble," he says, shaking his head. I can see that he's listening for something in the living room. He keeps straining his neck in that direction. "Trust me, I'm doing you a favor."

I want to tell him I get it, I've been married before, but I know he isn't here to commiserate. Who has the time? Certainly not me.

He checks his watch. "You should be dead already."

Believe me, I know.

"I'm sorry it's taking so long. I could put a bullet in you, but you see, I've already gone to all this trouble." He offers a pathetic frown, the kind that lets me know he isn't sorry at all. "I don't like to change things last minute. That's the sort of thing that gets you into trouble."

He leans down and uses the tip of his finger to pull my eyelid up. My eyes are open, and have been open, so I don't know why he insists on exposing my eyeball. I only know that I feel it moving in its socket and I'm trying desperately to close it. Bright light hits me and my eyelid strains against his fingers. "Aconite poisoning," he says like he's making a diagnosis. "Ten to one, that's what this is."

The light moves and I realize he's holding a flashlight. Better than the knife. I've already lost part of my tongue. I'd like to keep my eyes. "Can you hear me?" he calls, a little too jovial for my liking. It's the kind of tone that lets you know a person is batshit crazy.

"Hello? Anybody home?"

My throat is closing. I think this is it. This must be it.

"You'd think she'd learn. But she never does."

I feel myself being pulled under. The darkness is beckoning. It's too bad because I sort of want to hear what he has to say. I can't figure Ali out. He seems like the kind of guy with answers.

"All she had to do was stay home. Be a good wife. But no. Women these days. I swear nothing makes them happy."

I roll onto my side.

"Hey," he quips. "Where do you think you're going?" He peers into my face. He has the bluest eyes I've ever seen, but they're hollow and empty.

I roll again, giving it everything I've got. He comes for me and I use my feet against the counter to gain leverage. I roll a little farther this time. He thinks it's comical. That is, until I reach under the cabinet and grab the pistol I have hidden underneath and shoot him in the ankle. Blood spurts like a broken pipe, and it's really something. He's not laughing so much now. He falls and stabs at me with a knife I now see is from my own kitchen, which is a little annoying. Other than my car, those knives are the only thing I was awarded in my divorce.

It takes him several tries, but finally he contacts my thigh. I've just about got the gun aimed when the white-hot searing pain envelops me. He slides the knife out, and then there's more blood, and our blood mixes together, and it reminds me of being a kid, where you cut yourself to become blood brothers.

He pushes the knife in again. I feel it hit bone. It grazes along it, ripping and tearing through muscle achingly slowly. "And to think," he says. "All this time you had a gun. You should have said so. We could have made this so much easier."

He's right. I could have used the pistol on myself about five minutes ago, before he kicked in the door. I gave it serious consideration, anything to put myself out of this misery, but what a mess that would have been. A clean-up job on that level really affects the resale value of your home.

We wrestle a little more until we're both soaked and covered in blood. His uniform shirt is dunzo. It's definitely not coming back from this. All the blood on it looks like some weird art installation.

I finally free myself. He jumps off me and staggers backward. I finger the trigger and take aim. My second shot hits him in the shoulder. The rest hit center mass. He falls on top of me. I dip my finger in blood and write the word *aconite* across the white cabinet. Then everything goes black.

CHAPTER THIRTY-SEVEN

Ethan

I am the kind of sick where you wake up and don't remember it. The kind of sick where you come in and out of consciousness and days and time cease to exist. It's a strange feeling, knowing that you're on death's doorstep and it could go either way.

All I think about is how I ended up here.

Thankfully, Max visits and helps fill in the blanks. When Max visits, he tells me that when I stepped out to purchase the bottle of wine, Edward Kemp had doused my Italian meatballs with aconite.

"Ali is a vegetarian," he remarks as he sits at my bedside, fumbling with the TV remote. "Something that Edward Kemp knew, and you didn't. She never would have touched those meatballs."

"Apparently," I say. I speak with a terrible lisp. And probably will for some time. "Edward Kemp knew a lot of things."

"Sure did. He meticulously followed his wife's comings and goings."

"How?" I hate the way I sound, so I try to keep my answers short and sweet. I limit speaking at all whenever I can.

"Well, for one he studied the men she was involved with. He followed her. Often from city to city. He faked his injuries. Not all the injuries, just the extent of them. Then he murdered people, anyone who stood in his way. Sarah Shepard and Lucas Bennett included."

Max goes on to tell me that the day I planned to confront Ali, Edward had camped out in Kelsey's closet. He shakes his head. "We found a twelve-pack of bottled water and half a dozen protein bars. Cable ties, a stun gun, breath mints. Edward Kemp came prepared."

"He sure did."

"Mr. Stevens, your neighbor. The old man. You know the one?"

"I know Mr. Stevens."

"Well, his security camera showed Kemp crossing his lawn and walking straight into your garage. In the same frame, you're elbow deep in a flower bed."

"I had just finished mowing my yard. I had the garage open."

Max nods. "Yep."

"The stun gun and cable ties," I say. "Those he used on Ali. The breath mints and poison he reserved for me."

THE ROAD TO RECOVERY IS A LONG ONE. EVEN AFTER I AM released, I am incredibly weak. A shell of my former self. I spent thirteen days in the hospital, six of them on the brink of death. My quick thinking by writing the name of the herb that Edward Kemp used to poison me is what saved my life. That and having several handguns placed around my home, just in case. You learn a lesson once, it's best if you don't have to learn it again. If it hadn't been for the neighbor calling 911 after hearing shots fired, I would have died on the bathroom floor. But had it not been for Ali, I would have bled out long before the cops or paramedics arrived. I don't recall her tying the tourniquet around my leg. I had passed out well before then, but I'm told that she saved my leg, if not my life. What kind of woman can free herself from zip ties? If anyone can, I should have known it would be Ali.

I am released from the hospital on a Wednesday, my former least favorite day of the week. Bethany and the kids arrive to take me home. "You'll do anything to get out of therapy," she says, as she loads my belongings into her car.

I've been going to physical therapy at the hospital. I've learned to transfer from a wheelchair to a bed and the toilet, but it is my first time transferring to a car. I think of Edward Kemp and those photos and how only a crazy person could fake-live their life this way.

"You got this, Dad," Kelsey cheers as my arms shake. Nick holds the chair. I see him breathe a sigh of relief when I stick the landing, although when I turn to him, he manages a straight face.

"I was thinking I could stay over for a few days," Bethany tells me on the way home. "Help you get on your feet."

"It might be a while before that happens. Six weeks at least." I smile because I'm testing her. She'd kill me in the first twenty-four hours, and I might not mind. "Anyway, home healthcare is coming."

"Can we stay?" Kelsey asks.

Nick says, "It's Wednesday."

"It is Wednesday, isn't it," Bethany remarks, glancing over at me. "What do you think, Ethan? Are you up for company?"

I've never wanted anything more. "I'd love it."

I hadn't wanted to get poisoned or stabbed in the leg, but if it brings out this level of sympathy from my ex-wife, it's not quite so bad.

"Oh," Bethany says. "About Kelsey's birthday." She looks in the rearview mirror and then lowers her voice. "I've taken care of planning the party." She pats my thigh. The wounded one. "You have enough on your plate."

RECOVERY IS NOT ALL IT'S CRACKED UP TO BE. FOR THE FIRST FEW weeks, I wonder what the point of me pulling through was. It feels like a cruel, sick joke that I'm still alive, and I spend most of my days wondering why I bothered.

The cold sweats are horrible. The insomnia drives me mad. I have no appetite, so a home health aide comes daily, at least at first, and gives me nutrition through a tube in my stomach. They were able to sew my tongue back on and it takes several weeks before I can speak properly. And even then, in my mind, I no longer sound like myself.

The kids stayed over the first night, along with Max. Nadia stayed over for a few nights the first week. Then I was on my own.

Thankfully, Bethany brings the kids for regular visits. Nadia spends a large part of her day in my home office, working to keep the company afloat. Mostly, she's working insurance fraud cases, which she loves to hate. But thanks to the press the Kemp case gave us, we've been flush with business. Almost dying in order to solve a case, as it turns out, is a fairly good endorsement. Solving several additional murder cases in the process doesn't hurt either.

I'm glad for the work, even if it's my assistant taking the reins for the time being. It gives me something to look forward to in the future. For now, it's the people in my life that are keeping me alive.

Sometimes in moments of weakness, I open Beacon on my phone and read through old messages Ali sent. I look for her on the app, for a profile that sounds like something she would come up with, but she disappeared. I heard from Camille that Ali is staying in Boston, closing out her dead husband's affairs, which was difficult for Ali considering Edward Kemp's serial killer status, but Camille is happy. She finally received the green light for the insurance payout on her father, now that Edward Kemp has been named in his murder.

"I had my suspicions," Camille told me over the phone when she delivered the news. "My stepsister always hated my father. I didn't think she'd kill him, which is why I didn't mention her. Better to keep her name out of my mouth. I should have known better though. I'd put nothing past her. Whatever the case, she covered her tracks well. She married a sociopath."

"Rumor has it your father molested her."

"I begged my father not to marry her mother. Begged! I knew it was going to be a disaster from the start. Ali was always running around half-naked. She was always flaunting herself, parading around like a slut, from the first time I met her. But Daddy never would have touched her. Not unless Ali wanted it. Which, knowing her, she probably did."

I don't say anything. Because there isn't anything *to* say. It's funny how two people can see the same story very differently. Anything I might say wouldn't matter, anyway. Camille got what she wanted. She seems like the type of woman who always does.

Ali got her freedom.

"Here," Bethany says, tossing a piece of paper onto my lap. I let it flutter to the floor.

"Where are the kids?" I ask, looking toward the front window.

"I sent them for the mail. We need to talk."

I pick up the paper. It's a flyer.

"You look like shit," Bethany says as I stare at the words printed on the page.

I meet her eye and then crinkle the flyer into a ball and shoot it into the wastepaper basket across the room.

I miss.

She points at the crumbled paper on the floor. "You need that."

"*That,*" I say. "Is the last thing I need."

"You have eight weeks," she tells me. "Eight weeks to pull yourself together."

"We're divorced. It's a little late for ultimatums."

"Stop being a pussy, Ethan." She lays Kelsey's backpack on the couch beside me. "You'll need to help Kelsey with her math."

"Sure."

She glares at me for a long time. I listen for the kids, telepathically willing them to hurry. Bethany sighs. "Do it for them," she says, her eyes flitting toward the door when Kelsey and Nick come barreling through. "Do it for all of us who have to see you like this."

"I'm not doing it."

"Man up, okay."

I offer a tight smile and then turn my attention toward the door. Bethany is smart. She can take a hint. "Anything else?"

"Yes, as a matter of fact." She walks over and picks up the crumbled flyer and throws it at my head. "We need this just as much as you do. If not more. You have to get better."

CHAPTER THIRTY-EIGHT

Ali

Austin

Eight weeks later

Ali's excited about her workshop. It's been a while since she's set foot on a stage or stepped up to the podium, and God, has she missed it. Ali loves her work. She loves it even more since she's had to be away. It's given her a renewed sense of purpose, knowing there are so many women out there, many of them like she was until just recently, longing to be free.

It's an interesting thing, getting away with murder. It's gives you a certain, how do the French put it, a certain...*je ne sais quoi.*

Killing her stepfather was by far the most satisfying thing she's ever done. The fact that Edward helped, and inevitably took the fall, God, did that get her off. In more ways than one. She hadn't intended to have to assist with the disposal of Sarah Shepard, and yet she somehow found herself wrapped up in that when Edward refused to leave her body on the side of the road. He swore up and down that drivers who hit and run were usually caught, and he had no intention of going out like that. Ali did not let him off the hook easily. He paid for his actions dearly as she dangled Sarah's murder over his head. Thankfully, Edward's the only person who knows of her involvement and he's dead.

Edward brought crazy to a level of sexy that she's never seen. Unfortunately, he got greedy. He grew tired of their scams. Especially the one that kept him tied to a wheelchair. Ali sensed that he had improved beyond what he was letting on, but she wasn't certain. With Edward, she was never certain.

Seduction is an art. That was a gift that her husband taught her, and that's the topic of conversation at her lecture today. It's a packed house. There are easily three hundred people packed into the bookstore's large conference room. Ali stands and smooths her dress. The coordinator gives her the go-ahead as the event planner announces her. The woman lists off her accomplishments, awards, the titles of her books. Ali blushes and smiles shyly.

When Ali steps up to the podium, she adjusts the mic. She starts her talk with a question. *"How many of you have ever been seduced?* What was it about that time in your life that felt exciting?"

Ali knows the answer, of course, even if the audience can't quite put their finger on it.

It was the uncertainty. The highs and lows. The push and pull. Attraction without polarity cannot be sustained. Once the excitement is gone, you might as well just be friends. Friendship is fine. But that's not why her audience has come.

Ali shares her wisdom. She tells them there's power in

knowing how to seduce a person, and with that power must come respect. "So. You have this connection with this person. You must learn to hold it in your palm, like a sparrow. And trust that it will come back. Or it won't. Really. And if it doesn't, it's because that little bird did what it needed to do. And if it does, you will feed it from your open palm, and never close your fist around it. Then, it will know it's always safe with you. That is the ultimate seduction."

Once she's established ground rules, she moves to the next level. She teaches them about reading gestures and actions, about understanding a person's vulnerabilities in a way that would in turn help them read their partner's mind to glean insight into what their deepest desires are.

"For example," she says, moving away from the podium. "Let's say you're not in the mood for sex, or for Indian food, not *again*. But you realize that your partner is. Now—this is where it gets tricky. This is where I'm going to lose some of you." She steps forward. "If it were me, I'd make sure they get those things. Relationships are not fifty-fifty. Maybe a mediocre relationship. Show of hands. Who wants mediocre sex? Who came to learn about that? Who here wants a partner that's *maybe* a four? No one. Everyone wants a ten. But to get a ten—and to keep a ten—you have to be a ten. After all, you get what you give."

She tells them to be a storyteller if possible. There are few people on the planet who would turn down a truly emotional or romantic tale. Danger is an aphrodisiac, and it's difficult to convey danger if emotions aren't engaged.

Finally, she touches briefly on power dynamics and the best ways to bring them into the bedroom. A lot of conflict can be resolved between the sheets.

Or with murder. But it's probably better that Ali not say that.

She takes several questions from the audience. *How do I make sure I orgasm during sex? Does penis size really matter? Best sex position to hit the G-spot?* The usual. And then it's over. The audience gives a standing ovation.

Ali smiles and takes a bow. There's nothing quite like watching a group of men and women walk away armed with knowledge that will bring them pleasure. She searches the audience in the way that she always does at the end of a conference, reading faces, gauging levels of understanding and satisfaction.

Across the room, in the back row, her eyes land on a familiar face. She smiles. *It's him.*

CHAPTER THIRTY-NINE

Ethan

It's probably a beast better starved than fed, but the capacity we have to lie to ourselves is amazing. Plus, I've never been more attracted to her than right now seeing her on that stage. Ali's in her element. She's straight fire. Sexy as hell, a woman with ambition like that. I hadn't seen her at work before.

As I sit there watching her, I thank my lucky stars that Camille Roberts entered my life. I think about all the things that had to lead up to making that a possibility. My leaving the Bureau. Bethany's insistence that I start my own firm. The list goes on. I think about fate and how sometimes it hands you a gift and you realize the universe has a very interesting sense of humor. As much as we like to think we have all the answers, there's far more that's unexplainable. My attraction to this woman being one of those things. Life is a mystery. It doesn't come with neat and tidy answers. There are often more ellipses than full-on sentence stops.

I knew even before Bethany gave me the flyer for Ali's talk that I wouldn't miss it. Not for the world. I could lie to Bethany. I could lie to myself. Just not forever. And now here we are.

Ali finishes speaking and then spends half an hour chatting with attendees and signing books while I hang around browsing the bookstore. I pick up several books for the kids. When I finally make it to the biography section, I feel a tap on my shoulder. "Hello, stranger."

I turn, not expecting my breath to hitch in my throat. I am not expecting to want to push Ali up against the bookcase and go at it right there in the middle of a crowded store, but that's exactly what happens.

My mouth finds hers, and she goes with it, until someone clears their throat and Ali pulls away. We're both surprised by the man standing next to us. He wears nice clothes and a less than thrilled expression.

"Ethan," Ali says, "This is Michael Beck."

The man extends his hand, and I let it hang in the air for several seconds longer than necessary before taking it. "Ethan Lane."

"Ah," he says, shaking vigorously. "I've heard about you." He looks to Ali and then back at me. "You're the cop, right?"

I don't answer him. Ali does it for me. "Ethan's not a police officer. He's just an old friend."

"Guess I have the wrong guy."

He has no idea.

"You wanna grab a cup of coffee?" I say to Ali.

She looks at me and then turns to the chump standing opposite us. "Would you mind?"

"No, no," he tells her in a manner that lets me know they haven't been dating long. "Of course not."

"Perfect," Ali says, leaning forward to kiss his cheek. "I'll call you later?"

Beck nods. "It was nice meeting you."

I offer a terse smile. It's the least I can do.

Venturing outside, the sidewalk is teeming with people. The afternoon light is quickly fading. The buildings reflect the heat; mirroring the sky. The sun is still bright, and it's hot, typical of late June. It's my favorite time of year, stifling and wonderful.

"I hate summer," Ali says, slipping her arm through mine. "I've always hated summer."

"Where to?"

She leans into me comfortably. "There's a place I know around the corner."

"So this Beck guy...what's up with that? I thought you might be through running scams."

"You sound disappointed."

"Maybe a little."

"I like Michael."

I think of all the ways to make Michael disappear, but I'm comforted by the fact that Ali never keeps men around long. "You could do better."

"I've missed you," she says. "I wasn't sure I'd ever see you again."

"I don't believe that for a second."

She laughs. The only thing I love more than the month of June is hearing that laugh. Ali squeezes my arm. "You're right. I knew you couldn't stay away. Which is why I've been thinking—" She pauses and looks at me with a mischievous gleam in her eye. "I was thinking we should get a house out in the country. And maybe a couple of dogs...or a horse. I used to love horses."

I've always wanted to live in the country. But I don't say that. "A house in the country? What for?"

"I don't know. I guess so no one could hear you scream."

"That's not funny."

"Oh, Ethan," Ali says. "We could have such a damned good time together, don't you think?"

"Yes," I tell her, rounding the corner. "I think we could." I hold the cafe door open and motion with my hand. "It's just—"

"Just what?" She waits for me to answer before stepping inside.

"You said I wasn't your type. Remember? And then you almost got me killed."

"What can I say?" She shrugs. "Sometimes things start slow and they build."

CHAPTER FORTY

Ali

An undisclosed small town in Texas

December

E than stomps his feet on the doormat several times before crossing the threshold. Dirt flies everywhere. He looks up and meets her eye. "Don't worry," he says. "I'll clean it up."

Ali pulls the throw tighter around her shoulders. He's left the door open and the chill creeps in. Outside, the sun hangs low in the sky.

"You look comfy." He eases out of his boots and then warms his hands by the fire. "What have you been up to?"

"Oh, you know. A little of this, a little of that."

He tosses her a concerned look. "No, really."

"I wrote a little. I'm working on a new talk, something for my next conference. It feels promising."

She holds up a novel. He squints to see the cover. "And I just started reading this."

"*Kill Me Tomorrow*, huh." He rubs his jaw. "It looks interesting."

"It had better be. What else am I supposed to do here for six days?"

He walks over to her and plants a kiss directly on her mouth. "I can think of a few things."

It's their first Christmas in the old farmhouse, their first Christmas as a couple. Ethan spent the last four months restoring the place while Ali wrapped up business around the country. She closed her office in Seattle. Said she no longer liked the rain. And Boston, she said, was too cold. "The world is ripe with possibilities," she said to Ethan. "Sometimes you just need a fresh start."

Restoring the old house, a place Ali found outside of Austin, was that for him. Using his hands, teaching Kelsey and Nick about farm life, and watching them explore the place has afforded him a different way of looking at life. Which is to say, life goes on. No matter what, life goes on.

"You took forever," Ali says, laying the book aside. "Want some tea?"

"I'd love some." She watches him add logs to the fire. "Everything was packed. The tourists have officially arrived. First time I've ever seen traffic on Main Street. This town, with its three stoplights. You should have seen it. It was crazy."

She takes a knife from the base and slices into a lemon. "Tourists. I say we kill them all."

"Ah," he says, making his way into the kitchen. He wraps his arms around her waist. "There's the Christmas spirit. Unfortunately, they'll just keep coming."

"I didn't take you for a quitter." She fills two mugs with water from the kettle and drops the tea bags in. Then she turns to him and arches her brow suggestively. "So what now?"

"I could use a shower. Care to join me?"

"I've never wanted anything more. But it has to be quick. I have an appointment this evening. I have to drive back to the city."

"To Austin? No way."

"Yes way." She glances over her shoulder. "Now come on, before I change my mind."

Afterward, he studies her as she fastens her bra. His eyes do not leave her as she searches for her jeans, lingering still as she slides them over her thighs. "So, you really have to go."

She wraps the towel around her head and squeezes the excess water from her hair. But mostly, she ignores his question. "Have you seen the hair dryer?"

"Nope."

"Guess I'll have to rub two stones together. Or whatever they did in the olden days."

Ethan loves her optimism. He loves everything about her. "Or you could go sit by the fire I built. Or let it air dry. Stay here where it's warm."

"You know how it is. I get the call. I have to go."

"I do know." He sucks in his bottom lip. "But that doesn't mean I don't get to complain about it."

"There's nothing worse than a complainer." She scans the room, looking for the items that she had laid out on the bed. Items that were supposed to have made it into the dresser, but never did. Items that are now dispersed on the floor. "Especially at Christmas."

"It's not Christmas yet. I still have a few days."

Her brows raise. "Maybe I'll stay in the city until then."

"You could never stay away that long."

She rolls her eyes. "You're probably right."

"I thought you were going to stay here and work on your talk."

"I was. I am."

"And what about that riveting novel?"

"My other work comes first. I could be saving a family, Ethan. What's that worth to you?" She shakes her head. "Surely, a few hours of me being away."

"I miss you when you go."

Ali glances out the window and sighs. Nothing ever changes, not really. "You'll live."

She crosses the room in search of her favorite sweater. "And don't be such a baby. It's not like you."

"I'm not. I just thought I might get you all to myself for the holidays."

"Says the man who spent half the morning working. And, unfortunately, like criminals, relationship issues don't take holidays."

"So, this is what? An intervention?"

"Something like that."

Ethan shakes his head and searches for clothes. He throws on the first thing he can find. "I guess that happily ever after thing was all a lie."

Ali studies him carefully. "It seems you've forgotten how good I am at my job."

"I could never."

She watches him for a long moment as she chews at her lip, mulling over how much he ought to know. "It's Bethany."

"Bethany?"

"That's what I said."

"You're seeing my ex-wife?" Ethan thinks of the last time his ex saw another woman behind his back and considers how that turned out.

"Call it a favor." Ali slips the sweater over her head. "An early Christmas gift."

His face grows hot. "I couldn't give two shits about Bethany or her relationship issues. She made her bed—"

"But you forget your children share that bed."

Ethan stares at Ali for a long time. He hates when she does this. Uses logic to beat him at his own game.

Finally, he walks over to where she's sitting on the bed. He drops to the floor and takes her hand in his, intertwining their fingers, shifting his approach. "You're right. I'm sorry." He searches her face. "You're doing something kind and I'm being a shit."

"You don't say?" The way he looks at her causes memories of what they've just done to flood her mind. The shower tile cold against her back, the scalding water hitting her just right. The sounds of their pleasure heightened by the echo of the room.

"I picked up salmon," he tells her solemnly. "I wanted to give you your Christmas gift."

Her eyes narrow. She could stay and make him happy. She could use the internet to do the session. She could postpone it until morning. There are a million ways things could go, but all of them would all lead in the direction of her giving up what she really wants. Ali knows better. "How about a rain check?"

A wry smile lights up his features. "Fine." Ethan shakes his head and takes something from his pocket. "I guess you're going to be needing this."

He drops a tiny, clear thing into her hand.

"What—"

"It's a fuse. Your car won't start without it."

"My God. You're fucking crazy."

She sighs as he takes a fistful of hair and pulls her toward him. "Crazy about you, yes. How else was I supposed to make sure you didn't leave before I got back with dinner?"

"I can't believe you," she says, massaging her temples. Ethan's a pain in the ass, but the way he fucks makes up for it.

"Alas, my evil plan to keep you here has failed."

Ali pulls away and searches the dresser for her keys. Then remembers they were on top of her luggage, on the bed. "Marry better next time. And then I won't have to go fixing your problems."

"Bethany's problems aren't my problems. Not anymore."

He watches in amusement as she leans down and peers under the bed, thinking they could be anywhere in this mess. They're still in the process of getting the farmhouse situated. Ethan has his tools everywhere. Not that she'd complain. She appreciates a man who's handy.

"Looking for these," he calls from behind her. Ali practically jumps from her hands and knees. When she stands and turns, she freezes. Her first instinct is to hold her breath. And then she gasps, and all the air is expelled from her lungs. Ethan, on bended knee, smiles up at her, his expression devious. She sucks a deep breath in. They had a deal. They agreed to keep things light. Nothing serious. *This* is not that.

In his palm rests a small box with the lid open. Next thing she knows, he's shoving the perfect antique ring in her face.

"It was my grandmother's."

"Liar."

"Fine," he shrugs. "But do you like it?"

She exhales slowly, and as she does, her face softens. Not because she is happy, although she can easily pretend, but because it took him longer than she expected.

"Ali," he says, sucking in a deep breath. "I know it's only been what? Six months. I get it. Believe me, I know this is crazy. But who cares?" He nods toward the front door. "I have to ask. What do you know about caring for and feeding horses?"

She's speechless, although there is a lot she could tell him about her past, about her childhood. About growing up with horses and Donovan Robert's affinity for breeding them. But her clients are waiting. And the past should stay where it belongs, in the past. "Everything!" she squeals. "I know everything."

He stands and pulls her to him tightly, squeezing so hard it knocks the breath out of her. He slips the ring on her pinky finger. Better that way, than a *real* proposal. Men who propose to Ali end up dead and Ethan is quite happy with life these days.

"It's a pinky promise," she says, admiring the ring. It fits perfectly.

"So that's a yes, then?"

"Yes!"

"You have no idea—you've just made me the poorest man in the world. Horses are expensive."

He kisses her cheek first and then her mouth before nipping at her neck with his teeth. Ethan's mouth was very effective. The best. He's the kind of man who makes it obvious he's had a lot of practice, the kind who wastes no time. Which at the moment is perfect.

"Bethany will be fine," he murmurs against her skin. "I'm sure of it."

She doesn't argue because she understands.

"Let's go see a man about a horse, shall we?"

She winces. "First, I have a confession."

"Of course you do."

"I wasn't going into the city to counsel Bethany. I was going to pick up the kids. It was meant to be a surprise."

He takes her by the hand and leads her toward the door. When it opens, he points to his car. "I'm two steps ahead of you."

Kelsey and Nick are sitting there looking bored and annoyed. "You left them in the car?"

"I left the heat on. And they have internet. They'll survive."

She looks at him sideways. "We showered and everything."

"Yes," he smiles. "Much better to get that out of the way."

Ethan waves and the kids spill out of the car. Ali looks over at him. Children aren't her forte and it's obvious. She doesn't quite know how to be around them. "What now?"

"Now, we go down to the barn."

"And then what?"

He turns to her. "Your guess is a good as mine."

"No. Seriously."

"Maybe we'll go into town and scope out the tourist scene. See if anything interesting turns up."

Ali smiles mischievously. "Now, *that* is an idea I can work with."

A NOTE FROM BRITNEY

Dear Reader,

I hope you enjoyed reading *Kill Me Tomorrow.*

Writing a book is an interesting adventure, it's a bit like inviting people into your brain to rummage around. *Look where my imagination took me. These are the kind of stories I like...*

That feeling is often intense and unforgettable. And mostly, a ton of fun.

With that in mind—thank you again for reading my work. I don't have the backing or the advertising dollars of big publishing, but hopefully I have something better...readers who like the same kind of stories I do. If you are one of them, please share with your friends and consider helping out by doing one (or all) of these quick things:

1. Visit my review page and write a 30 second review (even short ones make a big difference).

(http://britneyking.com/aint-too-proud-to-beg-for-reviews/)

Many readers don't realize what a difference reviews make but they make ALL the difference.

2. Drop me an email and let me know you left a review. This way I can enter you into my monthly drawing for signed paperback copies.

(hello@britneyking.com)

3. Point your psychological thriller loving friends to their free copies of my work. My favorite friends are those who introduce me to books I might like. **(http://www.britneyking.com)**

4. If you'd like to make sure you don't miss anything, to receive an email whenever I release a new title, sign up for my new release newsletter.

(https://britneyking.com/new-release-alerts/)

Thanks for helping, and for reading my work. It means a lot.

Britney King

Austin, Texas

March 2021

ABOUT THE AUTHOR

Britney King lives in Austin, Texas with her husband, children, a dog named Gatsby, one ridiculous cat, and a partridge in a peach tree.

When she's not wrangling the things mentioned above, she writes psychological, domestic and romantic thrillers set in suburbia.

Without a doubt, she thinks connecting with readers is the best part of this gig. You can find Britney online here:

Email: britney@britneyking.com
Web: https://britneyking.com
Facebook: https://www.facebook.com/BritneyKingAuthor
Instagram: https://www.instagram.com/britneyking_/
Twitter: https://twitter.com/BritneyKing_
Goodreads: https://bit.ly/BritneyKingGoodreads
Pinterest: https://www.pinterest.com/britneyking_/

Happy reading.

ACKNOWLEDGMENTS

Many thanks to my family and friends for your support in my creative endeavors.

To the beta team, ARC team, and the bloggers, thank you for making this gig so much fun.

Last, but not least, thank you for reading my work. Thanks for making this dream of mine come true.

I appreciate you.

Speak of the Devil | Book Three

The New Hope Series Box Set

The New Hope Series offers gripping, twisted, furiously clever reads that demand your attention, and keep you guessing until the very end. For fans of the anti-heroine and stories told in unorthodox ways, *The New Hope Series* delivers us the perfect dark and provocative villain. The only question—who is it?

Water Under The Bridge | Book One

Dead In The Water | Book Two

Come Hell or High Water | Book Three

The Water Series Box Set

The Water Trilogy follows the shady love story of unconventional married couple—he's an assassin—she kills for fun. It has been compared to a crazier book version of Mr. and Mrs. Smith. Also, Dexter.

Bedrock | Book One

Breaking Bedrock | Book Two

Beyond Bedrock | Book Three

The Bedrock Series Box Set

The Bedrock Series features an unlikely heroine who should have known better. Turns out, she didn't. Thus she finds herself tangled in a messy, dangerous, forbidden love story and face-to-face with a madman hell-bent on revenge. The series has been compared to Fatal Attraction, Single White Female, and Basic Instinct.

Around The Bend

Around The Bend, is a heart-pounding standalone which traces the journey of a well-to-do suburban housewife, and her life as it unravels, thanks to the secrets she keeps. If she were the only one with things she

wanted to keep hidden, then maybe it wouldn't have turned out so bad.
But she wasn't.

Somewhere With You / Book One

Anywhere With You / Book Two

The With You Series Box Set

The With You Series at its core is a deep love story about unlikely friends
who travel the world; trying to find themselves, together and apart.
Packed with drama and adventure along with a heavy dose of suspense, it
has been compared to The Secret Life of Walter Mitty and Love, Rosie.

GET EXCLUSIVE MATERIAL

Looking for a bit of dark humor, chilling deception and enough suspense to keep you glued to the page? If so, tap the image or click here to receive your starter library. Easy peasy.

SNEAK PEEK: THE SOCIAL AFFAIR

BOOK ONE

In the tradition of *Gone Girl* and *Behind Closed Doors* comes a gripping, twisted, furiously clever read that demands your attention, and keeps you guessing until the very end. For fans of the antiheroine and stories told in unorthodox ways, *The Social Affair* delivers us the perfect dark and provocative villain. The only question—who is it?

A timeless, perfect couple waltzes into the small coffee shop where Izzy Lewis works. Instantly enamored, she does what she always does in situations like these: she searches them out on social media.

Just like that—with the tap of a screen— she's given a front row seat to the Dunns' picturesque life. This time, she's certain she's found what she's been searching for. This time, she'll go to whatever lengths it takes to ensure she gets it right—even if this means doing the unthinkable.

Intense and original, The Social Affair is a disturbing psychological thriller that explores what can happen when privacy is traded for convenience.

What readers are saying:

"Another amazingly well-written novel by Britney King. It's every bit as dark, twisted and mind twisting as Water Under The Bridge...maybe even a little more so."

"Hands down- best book by Britney King. Yet. She has delivered a difficult writing style so perfectly and effortlessly, that you just want to worship the book for the writing. The author has managed to make murder/assassination/accidental- gunshot- to-the-head-look easy. Necessary."

"Having fallen completely head over heels for these characters and this author with the first book in the series, I've been pretty much salivating over the thought of this book for months now. You'll be glad to know that it did not disappoint!"

Praise

"If Tarantino were a woman and wrote novels... they might read a bit like this."

"Fans of Gillian Flynn and Paula Hawkins meet your next obsession."

"Provocative and scary."

"A dark and edgy page-turner. What every good thriller is made of."

"I devoured this novel in a single sitting, absolutely enthralled by the storyline. The suspense was clever and unrelenting!"

"Completely original and complex."

"Compulsive and fun."

"No-holds-barred villains. Fine storytelling full of mystery and suspense."

"Fresh and breathtaking insight into the darkest corners of the human psyche."

THE SOCIAL AFFAIR

BRITNEY KING

THE
SOCIAL
AFFAIR

A NOVEL

BRITNEY KING

COPYRIGHT

Hot Banana Press

Cover Design by Britney King LLC

Cover Image by Mario Azzi

Copy Editing by Librum Artis Editorial Services

Proofread by Proofreading by the Page

First Edition: 2018

ISBN 13: 978-1979057455

ISBN 10: 1979057451

britneyking.com

To those who've walked into our lives without first asking permission...

PROLOGUE

Attachment is an awfully hard thing to break. I should know. I surface from the depths of sleep to complete and utter darkness. I don't want to open my eyes. I have to. "I warned you, and I warned you," I hear his voice say. It's not the first time. He called out to me, speaking from the edge of consciousness, back when I thought this all might have been a dream. It's too late for wishful thinking now. This is his angry voice, the one I best try to avoid. My mind places it immediately. This one is reserved for special occasions, the worst of times.

I hear water running in the background. Or at least I think I do. For my sake, I hope I'm wrong. I try to recall what I was doing before, but this isn't that kind of sleep. It's the heavy kind, the kind you wake from and hardly know what year you're in, much less anything else. I consider how much time might have passed since I dozed off. Then it hits me.

"You really shouldn't have done that," he says, and his eyes come into focus. Those eyes, there's so much history in them; it's all still there now. I see it reflected back to me. I read a quote once that said... a true mark of maturity is when someone hurts you, and you try to understand their situation instead of trying to hurt them back. This seems idealistic now. I wish someone had warned me. Enough of that kind of thinking will get you killed.

"Please," I murmur, but the rest of what I want to say won't come. It's probably better this way. I glance toward the door, thinking about what's at stake if I don't make it out of here alive, wondering whether or not I can make a break for it. It's so dark out—a clear night, a moonless sky. The power is out, I gather, and it's a fair assumption. This has always been one of his favorite ways to show me what true suffering is like. That alone would make an escape difficult. I would have to set out on foot and then where would I go? Who would believe me?

"You have it too easy," he says, as though he wants to confirm my suspicions. "That's the problem nowadays. People consume everything, appreciate nothing."

He lifts me by the hair and drags me across the bedroom. I don't have to ask why. He doesn't like to argue where he sleeps, where we make love. It's one of our safe spaces, but like many things, this too is a facade. Nothing with him is safe.

"You like your comforts, but you forget nothing good comes without sacrifice."

"I haven't forgotten," I assure him, and that much is true. Sacrifice is something I know well.

He shakes his head, careful to exaggerate his movements. He wants the message he sends to sink in. "I don't know why you have to make me so angry."

I glance toward the window, thinking I see headlights, but it's wishful thinking. Then I reach up and touch the wet spot at the crown of my head. I pull my hand away, regretful I felt the need for confirmation. Instinct is enough. If only I'd realized this sooner. I didn't have to put my fingers to it to know there would be blood; the coppery scent fills the air. "It's not too bad," he huffs as he slides one hand under my armpit and hauls me up. "Come on," he presses, his fingertips digging into my skin. "Let's get you stitched up."

I follow his lead. There isn't another option. Head wounds bleed a lot, and someone's going to have to clean his mess up. If I live, that someone will be me. *This is how you stop the bleeding.* "What time is it?"

"Oh," he says, half-chuckling. "There's no need to worry about that. She's already come and gone."

I don't ask who he's referring to. I know. Everything in me sinks to the pit of my stomach. It rests there and I let it. I don't want him to see how deeply I am affected by what he's done. It's more dangerous if I let it show. But what I want to happen and what actually does, are two very different things. I know because my body tenses, as it gives over to emotion until eventually it seizes up completely. I don't mean for it to happen. It has a habit of betraying me, particularly where he is concerned. Your mind may know when something's bad for you. But the body can take a little longer. He knows where to touch me. He knows what to say. Automatic response is powerful, and like I said before, attachment is hard to break.

He shoves me hard into the wall. I guess I wasn't listening. I shouldn't have made a habit of that either. I don't feel the pain. I don't feel anything. "Ah, now look what you made me do," he huffs, running his fingers through his hair. He's staring at me as though this is the first time he's seeing me. His face is twisted. He wants me to think he's trying to work out his next move. He isn't. He's a planner, through and through.

Still, he's good at concealing what he doesn't want anyone to know. If only I'd been more like that. I wasn't. That's why I don't know if this is it, if this is the end. I only know where it began.

"We had an agreement," he reminds me. And he's right.

We did have an agreement.

That's how this all started.

READ MORE HERE: https://books2read. com/b/thesocialaffair

Made in the USA
Las Vegas, NV
11 April 2021

21214729R00155